# The Awe & Wonder of Jesus

**The Greatest love story ever told**
**By:   Rodney Halford**

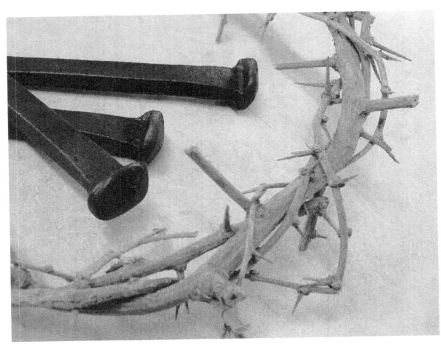

## IGNITE THE FIRE

www.ignitethefireministry.com

ISBN: 9798435455724

Imprint: Independently published

# Table of Contents

**I would like to dedicate this book to the following people:**

My wife Kelly. You are an amazing wife & mother. Your love for Jesus, your children, your family, and me is absolutely amazing! You are my better half. God loved me so much he took the time to create you just for me. Thank you for all your love, your support, and your pushing me to be a better man.

To my kids, Jacob, Christian, & Elijah. I hope this book is a part of my legacy for you. I want to pass on this heart for Jesus on to you. I want you to love Him even more than I do. He loves you more than I could ever describe to you. Hopefully as you read this, you will realize how much he truly does love you.

These people honor me only with their words, for their hearts are so very distant from me. They pretend to worship me, but their worship is nothing more than the empty traditions of men."


Matthew 15:8-9

"The Bible is the story of two gardens: Eden and Gethsemane. In the first, Adam took a fall. In the second, Jesus took a stand. In the first, God sought Adam. In the second, Jesus sought God. In Eden, Adam hid from God. In Gethsemane, Jesus emerged from the tomb. In Eden, Satan led Adam to a tree that led to his death. From Gethsemane, Jesus went to a tree that led to our life."

- **Max Lucado**

# Introduction

I am not a writer. Let me say that again. **I am not a writer.** Not by any stretch of the imagination. Math has always been my strength. English and Grammar have always been my weaknesses. If you are reading this book expecting some great piece of literature, you will be disappointed in that regard. When the Lord put it on my heart to write this book, I have to admit, I laughed. I said, "Lord, I think you have the wrong one." If He needed some calculations done, I'm His man. Not writing. Not me. Beyond Math and English, I am not the best person to write on any subject, at least in my mind. That is what the enemy tells so many of us.

I knew that Jesus would give me the words, I just had to be a willing vessel. So I put together a list of areas to write about then I started writing. Each chapter I wanted to focus on Jesus. The beauty that is Him. I personally believe many of us have lost that deep, deep love for Him. A love so deep that you cannot live without Him. A love so strong you don't even want to take another breath without being closer to Him. I need Him, every moment of every day. He is not a Sunday morning love for me. He is the center of my life and without Him, everything is lost. I could never worship Him enough. I could never tell Him enough that I love Him.

He gave everything for us and we should do the same for Him. Jesus is not an ATM machine that we put our prayer in the little slot, ask Him for something, and expect it to be given to us. He is our God. He is our King. He is on the throne and deserves our Honor, our praise, and all the glory we can give him. When was the last time you went into your prayer closet, prayed, and didn't ask Him for anything personal? I encourage you to try that. Go into your prayer room, and tell Jesus, "Lord, I am here for you. There may be needs in my life, but right now, I am here for you." That is not to say Jesus doesn't want to hear you ask something of Him. However, it is an opportunity to state that Jesus is the only one that matters. Jesus is the center of it all. He holds it all together. It is all about you Jesus!

The things that Jesus did here on Earth defy logic. It defied reason. It defied the teachings of the Jewish leaders. The world saw his love and compassion on full display. The world would never be the same. What he did was a statement of that love for us. That statement was powerful. That statement was life-changing for millions throughout all time. Once you taste his love, his compassion, his mercy, and his power, you will never be the same!

My hope and prayer is that this book blesses you. Restores the Awe and Wonder of Jesus in your life. When we have that Awe and Wonder of Jesus, expectation of Him grows. When we have that

Awe and Wonder of Jesus, our love of Him grows. When we have that Awe and Wonder of Jesus, miracles happen. When we have that Awe and Wonder of Jesus, lives are changed, When we have that Awe and Wonder of Jesus, our worship changes. When we have that Awe and Wonder of Jesus, church services go from ordinary to extraordinary.

I hope that the fire inside you is ignited for Jesus. He is our only hope. Once done with this book, pass it on. Let it ignite another's fire and passion for Jesus!

## 1

## Mary, Mother of Jesus, His Birth, and Jesus at 12

Mary, mother of Jesus. Virgin. Engaged to be married to Joseph, a true descendant of King David. Living in Nazareth. God saw her as pure and righteous. Mary ended up pregnant with The King of Kings. The Messiah. The very Son of God. Amazing!

*Luke 1- TPT During the sixth month of Elizabeth's pregnancy, the angel Gabriel was sent from God's presence to an unmarried girl named Mary, living in Nazareth, a village in Galilee. She was engaged to a man named Joseph, a true descendant of King David.* [28] *Gabriel appeared to her and said, "Rejoice, beloved young woman, for the Lord is with you and you are anointed with great favor."*

[29] *Mary was deeply troubled over the words of the angel and bewildered over what this may mean for her.* [30] *But the angel reassured her, saying, "Do not yield to your fear, Mary, for the Lord has found delight in you and has chosen to surprise you with a wonderful gift.* [31] *You will become pregnant with a baby boy, and you are to name him Jesus.* [32] *He will be supreme and will be known as the Son of the Highest. And the Lord God will enthrone him as*

*King on the throne of his ancestor David. ³³ He will reign as King of Israel forever, and his reign will have no limit."*

*³⁴ Mary said, "But how could this happen? I am still a virgin!"*

*³⁵ Gabriel answered, "The Spirit of Holiness will fall upon you and almighty God will spread his shadow of power over you in a cloud of glory! This is why the child born to you will be holy, and he will be called the Son of God. ³⁶ What's more, your aged aunt, Elizabeth, has also become pregnant with a son. The 'barren one' is now in her sixth month. ³⁷ Not one promise from God is empty of power. Nothing is impossible with God!"*

*³⁸ Then Mary responded, saying, "Yes! I will be a mother for the Lord! As his servant, I accept whatever he has for me. May everything you have told me come to pass." And the angel left her.*

I can only imagine. Mary, a young Jewish girl. She was engaged to marry Joseph, a righteous man. God selected her to carry His son. The Son of the Living God. The Holy one. The Anointed One. The baby Jesus growing inside her. I am blown away that God would send His son to Earth to die for us. He was born to be a reflection of His glory. He was sent to show us His love for all of us. How great can a love be to send His only Son knowing what He is going to go through? Overwhelming. As a father of 3 sons, I could not even imagine doing that for mankind. He did that knowing how mankind would turn out. He knew how many horrible people there were going to be. Child molesters, murderers, rapists, terrorists. He knew. He knew all the mockers, the ones that could care less about Him. He knew what the world would become but His love for us all is so overwhelming, He gave it all. He paid the ultimate price for us. For you. For me.

Mary was carrying the baby that would change the world. Forever. She was with child. A child that would die for the sins of the world. He would right so many things that went wrong. He would bring hope to countless people. When Mary kissed the face of Jesus, she kissed the face of God. She was carrying the prophecy fulfilled throughout the Old Testament. In Isaiah 7:14, the Bible says,*"Therefore the Lord himself will give you a sign: The virgin will conceive and give birth to a son, and will call him Immanuel"* She was pregnant with the one who would heal countless people. The one who would walk on water, the one who calmed the seas. The one who cast out demons. Mary was so blessed that she was able to see the very face of God each and every day as Jesus grew up.

She got to see Him take his 1st step. She got to see Him speak His first words. I wonder, what were Jesus's first words when he was an infant? I wonder, did He heal when he was a toddler? An adolescent? A tweener? A teenager? Did he heal Mary or Joseph when they were sick? I wonder, what was going through Mary's head when she had to tell Joseph about Jesus, the angel appearing before her, and who the angel said he was? What was going through Joseph's head when the angel appeared to Him? I would bet there was some unbelief. Some thoughts of "am I crazy?" After all, this was totally against nature.

Who would believe that an angel appeared? Who would believe that the person you are engaged to get married to is pregnant with the Son of God? What level of faith would you have to have in order to believe this? After all, this is Nazareth. Who would come from Nazareth? How amazing, overwhelming is it to hear the angel of the Lord say that God finds favor in you? I wonder, did Mary fall to the ground, hearing that the Holy God of Israel, finds favor in her? Words can not even describe how a person would feel being told this. Then to be told that you are pregnant, without being with a man, with the Holy One. The Messiah. The Son of the Living God. The one that is going to change the world for generations to come and to the end of the world. Simply overwhelming.

I wonder, did Mary know what Jesus was going to go through when she was pregnant? When she was seeing Him grow up, did she know? Did she know how many lives he would change? Did she know how many healings he would perform? How many people were raised from the dead? How many demons he would cast out? Did she worship Him as a baby? As an infant, toddler, teenager? Jesus was on the Earth. God's only Son, all his majesty, all his glory, all his holiness, had come down to save us all. Mary got to see Him every day. How much anticipation did she have to see what He is going to do? To hear of the miracles He was going to do.

Did she truly understand who and what she was holding in her hands? Immanuel, meaning God with us. Wise men traveled from far to worship Him. A baby. They brought gifts. Strangers brought gifts to Mary and Joseph. They fell down and worshiped baby Jesus. They brought Him gifts. Incredible! They followed a star to find baby Jesus. Awesome! How important was He? Herod murdered every male child 2 years and younger in Israel. They feared Him even before He was born. They feared losing their power, their control over people. Losing their place in their religious leadership. Losing the power over their slaves. It is truly a reflection of the modern day. Leaders, politicians, and more with all their power and their biggest fear, losing that power. Religious leaders trying to look all Holy, all perfect, and their biggest fear, not looking Holy, righteous, and the stature that comes with it.

Jesus coming to this Earth, being born was the greatest point in history up to that time. The God that created the Heavens and Earth. The God who created man. The God who controls the sun, the moon, and the stars. The God who created every living thing. He sent His Son, as a demonstration of His love for us. Absolutely amazing! Words in the English language cannot even begin to describe that level of love. The Gospels are filled with examples of Jesus's love and compassion for us. He deserves all our praise, all our worship, all our love that we can pour out on Him. Every day!

Then there was the story of Jesus at 12 years old. It was Passover. As it was their custom, Mary and Joseph went to Jerusalem to observe the Passover. As they journeyed home, they realized Jesus was missing. They thought He was in their entourage, but He was not. They searched their family and friends. They went back to Jerusalem to search. 3 days later, Jesus was nowhere to be found. Finally, they found Him. 3 days. A 12-year-old child was missing for 3 days.

*Luke 2- TPT* *Every year Jesus' parents went to worship at Jerusalem during the Passover festival.* *42 When Jesus turned twelve, his parents took him to Jerusalem to observe the Passover, as was their custom.* *43 A full day after they began their journey home, Joseph and Mary realized that Jesus was missing.* *44 They had assumed he was somewhere in their entourage, but he was nowhere to be found. After a frantic search among relatives and friends,* *45 Mary and Joseph returned to Jerusalem to search for him.* *46 After being separated from him for three days, they finally found him in the temple, sitting among the Jewish teachers, listening to them and asking probing questions.* *47 All who heard Jesus speak were awestruck at his intelligent understanding of all that was being discussed and at his wise answers to their questions.*

*48 His parents were shocked to find him there, and Mary scolded him, saying, "Son, your father and I have searched for you everywhere! We have been worried sick over not finding you. Why would you do this to us?"*

*49 Jesus said to them, "Why would you need to search for me? Didn't you know that it was necessary for me to be here in my Father's house, consumed with him?"*

*50 Mary and Joseph didn't fully understand what Jesus meant.*

*51 Jesus went back home with them to Nazareth and was obedient to them. His mother treasured Jesus' words deeply in her heart. 52 As Jesus grew, so did his wisdom and maturity. The favor of men increased upon his life, for he was greatly loved by God.*

Jesus was in the temple, preaching. He was 12. He was TWELVE and preaching in the temple! What a story. I just can't stop thinking about it. He was TWELVE years old and preaching in the temple. That, in itself, is amazing! Let's take it a little further though. Jesus was, in the people's eyes, the son of a poor carpenter. The Bible says the people were awestruck by his intelligence. He was 12. He observed all the Jewish traditions, but he was not educated by traditional means. The only explanation was the words, the message was directly from God. I wonder, did anyone there think that he could possibly be the Messiah they had been waiting on? If so, what were they thinking, seeing the very Son of God standing in the Temple preaching? Did they take notes? (I know, I am being funny) I am pretty sure you couldn't take it all in. No cameras to record the teaching. Were they so awestruck they couldn't really listen to the words He was saying? What did He preach about? Were they Pharisees and scribes there? If so, what did they think? Were they offended like they were as he got older?

The awe and wonder of Jesus as a baby and as a 12-year-old is absolutely incredible! Their faith in believing the baby was the Son of God was astonishing. The people in the temple listen to a 12-year-old teaching. Wisemen come from afar to worship Him. The Wise Men, knowing who He is, knowing what Herod wanted to do to Him, did not report back to Herod. The Angel of the Lord tells Mary and Joseph to flee to Egypt for safety and in turn bring forth biblical prophecy from the Old Testament. In Hosea 11:1, the Bible says, *"When Israel was a child, I loved him, and out of Egypt I called my son."* Jesus was no ordinary child. He was no ordinary tweener or teenager. He had a mission, a Godly purpose that was going to be fulfilled. Mary, Joseph, the Wise Men, and more did many things to keep Him safe, keep His purpose safe, and what they did impacted the world then, and throughout all time. This is where our awe and wonder of Jesus as a baby & child comes into our lives today. We can truly learn from this. Following God's direction can and will impact generations upon generations.

## 2

## Baptism and the Wilderness

"Behold, the Lamb of God." Those words were uttered by John the Baptist when he saw Jesus. Jesus was coming to get baptized with everyone else, but this was more. This was more than a man being baptized. This was the very Son of God.

***John 1- TPT*** *Now this was John's testimony when some of the Jewish leaders sent an entourage of priests and temple servants[j] from Jerusalem to interrogate him. "Who are you?" they asked him.*

*20 John answered them directly, saying, "I am not the Messiah!"*
*21 "Then who are you?" they asked. "Are you Elijah?"*
*"No," John replied. So, they pressed him further, "Are you the prophet Moses said was coming, the one we're expecting?"*
*"No," he replied.*
*22 "Then who are you?" they demanded. "We need an answer for those who sent us. Tell us something about yourself—anything!"*
*23 John answered them, "I am an urgent, thunderous voice crying out in the desert—clear the way and prepare your hearts for the coming of the Lord Yahweh!"*

*24 Then some members of the religious sect known as the Pharisees questioned John, 25 "Why do you baptize the people if you are neither the Messiah, Elijah, nor the Prophet?"*

*26–27 John answered them, "I baptize the people in this river, but the One who will take my place is to be more honored than I, but even when he stands among you, you will not recognize or embrace him! I am not worthy enough to stoop down in front of him and untie his sandals!" 28 All these events took place at Bethany, where John was baptizing at the place of the crossing of the Jordan River.*

*29 The very next day, John saw Jesus coming to him to be baptized, and John cried out, "Look! There he is—God's Lamb! He takes away the sin of the entire world! 30 I told you that a Mighty One would come who is far greater than I am, because he existed long before I was born! 31 My baptism was for the preparation of his appearing to Israel, even though I didn't recognize him."*

*32 Then, as he baptized Jesus, he proclaimed these words: "I see the Spirit of God appear like a dove descending from the heavenly realm and landing upon him—and it remained on him! 33 Before this I didn't know who he was. But the one who sent me to baptize with water had told me, 'You will see the Spirit come down and stay on someone. He will be the One I have sent to baptize with the Holy Spirit.' 34 Now I have seen this happen and I can tell you for sure that this man is the Son of God.*

I imagine it was an ordinary day. A day of John the Baptist preaching, baptizing many, and turning many people to the Lord God Almighty. Then Jesus came. John the Baptist spoke about the coming Lord. He talked about the Messiah coming. He said someone greater than he was coming. Someone who he wasn't even worthy enough to be His slave. John the Baptist knew.

I wonder, what did John the Baptist think when he saw Jesus. He got to look upon the Holy One. The very Son of God standing in front of Him. How did he not fall to his knees? How did he not start worshiping Him right then and there? He was standing right in front of Jesus. I wonder, what did the others think when they watched as John the Baptist proclaimed Him to be the very Lamb of God? I know the Bible says Simon and Andrew immediately followed Him but what did the others think? What did they all think when they all heard God's voice say "This is my beloved Son, in whom I am well pleased in." God's voice. The voice of God. The audible voice of God. Think about that. Simply amazing. Incredible. How would you feel if you were talking to friends or at church and they all hear the voice of God saying he is well pleased with you? I don't know about you but I long for that. I long for God to say he is pleased with me. That is all I want is to please Him! I live to please Him. I live to serve Him!

After Jesus's baptism, he was immediately taken into the wilderness. After He fasted forty days and forty nights, Satan appeared to Him. He tempted Him 3 different ways. Satan tempted Him with food. He said if He was the Son of God, command these stones to become bread. Jesus replied, "For it is written, man shall not live by bread alone, but by every word that proceeds out of the mouth of God." Then Satan took Jesus, took Him up into the Holy city and set him on the top of the temple. Satan said, "If You are the Son of God, throw yourself down. For it is written, He shall give His angels charge over you. In their hands they shall bear you up, lest you dash your foot against a stone." Then Jesus said, "It is written again, you shall not tempt the Lord your God." For the third and final one, Satan took him up on a mountain, and showed Him all the kingdoms of the world and their glory. Then Satan said, "All of these things I will give you if you will fall down and worship me." Then Jesus said unto him "Away with you Satan! For it is written, you shall worship the Lord your God, and Him only shall you serve." Jesus sent Satan packing. He was running away like the nothing he is.

There are several things to talk about here. What did the people there at the baptism think when they saw Jesus disappear? I can imagine they were very awestruck. 40 days without food? The Bible says afterwards he hungered. That, in itself, leaves me awestruck. Therefore, Satan's first temptation was food. But let's go a little deeper into this. You notice that each time Satan says, "If you are the Son of God." He was not saying this in terms of reassurance that He was the Son of God. He was trying to put doubt in Jesus's mind that He was who He was. Satan will always try to put doubt in Christian's minds of who they are in Christ.

Wouldn't you know it, the very weakest point in Jesus to that point in His life, right on cue, here comes the enemy. He loves to try to come and stir up trouble. In my mind, Satan's very appearance before Jesus is a testimony of who he was and what He was about to do. He knew who He was. He even had the nerve to try to quote scripture, to Jesus. He quoted scripture to Jesus. How hilarious is that? I also find it funny that his first temptation was for Jesus to turn rocks into bread. He's Jesus. If he wanted bread, don't you think He could create bread? I know, it was about his obedience to God but He could have if he wanted to.

Then Satan asked Him to throw Himself down in Jerusalem. Really? How dumb is he? If Jesus really wanted to, he could have called angels and left the Earth. I imagine he was trying to get Jesus to believe that the people would believe in Him if they saw the angels catching Him. In reality, again, to be disobedient, go against God's will, and choose to do something he thought would be better. Right. The very Son of God is going to do something against His Father's will. Then for his third try, Satan tried to give

Jesus all the kingdoms of the Earth. Again, how dumb is he? Jesus already has all the kingdoms of the Earth.

I know, I am making light of the whole thing. In reality, I can imagine that is what Jesus is thinking though. How could Satan be that dumb? Does he really think he could give Jesus something that Jesus could create on His own? Does he really think Jesus, the Son of God, is going to jump off the Temple to show people who he is? Does he really think he could offer Jesus kingdoms that he very soon will not own? I love how in the end Jesus sent him away. He completed the 3 temptations by running him off. I can only imagine how hungry and tired Jesus was. Yes, he was the Son of God, but he was also flesh. A man. How hungry would a person be after forty days of not eating? How weak would a person's body be after not having nourishment for forty days? Then you add in being alone, in the wilderness. Probably very hot. I imagine there were opportunities to eat there during the forty days.

My Awe and wonder moment here was that Jesus was obedient to His Father through it all. He was going to accomplish everything that God wanted. His determination was incredible. His determination was fueled by his desire to fulfill God's plan and His love for us. His love was and is so strong for us that he was not going to fail. He was not going to get sidetracked. He was going to fulfill His Father's will no matter what. He willingly went through everything He went through for us. Talk about the awe and wonder of Jesus. Throughout all time, Jesus loved us so much that he did all that he did. He could have said we are not worth it. He could have said, why bother? Look at the world 2000 years later. All the hatred. All the violence. All the horrible people. The crooked politicians. The crooked ministers. The Christians who could care less about me. He saw the good in us. He saw what we could be if we give everything to Him. After all, how could he ask us to give everything if He doesn't? On the flip side of that, how could we not give everything, knowing he gave it all?

## 3

## Water into wine and the living water

Up to this point, Jesus tried to keep quiet about who he really was. He kept saying His time has not yet come. That was all about to change. There was a wedding planned in Cana. Mary, Jesus's mother and his entire family was attending. It was a grand celebration. Wine, dancing, more wine. Back then, they would serve the absolute best wine first, then move into a lesser wine as people drank. Then comes the problem. They are out of wine. What? How is that possible? Did they have more guests than anticipated? Did they drink more than anticipated? This is a huge issue as the people that were putting the wedding on did not want to look foolish in front of everyone.

Jesus was about to be revealed as the Messiah, the living hope for mankind. Everything is about to change!

*John 2 Now on the third day, Jesus' mother went to a wedding feast in the Galilean village of Cana. 2-3 Jesus and his disciples were all invited to the banquet, but with so many guests, they ran out of wine. And when Mary realized it, she came to Jesus and asked, "They have no wine; can't you do something about it?"*

*4 Jesus replied, "My dear one, don't you understand that if I do this, it will change nothing for you, but it will change everything for me! My hour of unveiling my power has not yet come."*

*5 Mary then went to the servers and told them, "Whatever Jesus tells you, do it!"*

*6 Nearby stood six stone water pots meant to be used for the Jewish washing rituals. Each one could hold about twenty gallons or more. 7 Jesus came to the servers and instructed them, "Fill the pots with water, right up to the very brim." 8 Then he said, "Now fill your pitchers and take them to the master of ceremonies."*

*9 And when they poured out their pitchers for the master of ceremonies to sample, the water had become wine! When he tasted the water that had become wine, the master of ceremonies was impressed with its quality. (Although he didn't know where the wine had come from, only the servers knew.) He called the bridegroom over 10 and said to him, "Every host serves his best wine first, until everyone has had a cup or two, then he serves the cheaper wine. But you, my friend, you've reserved the most exquisite wine until now!"*

*11 This miracle in Cana was the first of the many extraordinary miracles Jesus performed in Galilee that revealed his glory, and his disciples believed in him.*

Then Mary, Jesus's mother, thought about the fact that the problem solver is there. Jesus. He could help. What would Jesus do? He's a carpenter's son. From Nazareth. Poor Nazareth. What could he do about the lack of wine? I imagine there were many thoughts like that there. Many of them snickering, whispering, laughing. Would he go find more wine? Would he find someone that could get more wine? Those are two more obvious solutions. However, that night, there was something greater happening. It was a coming out party for Jesus. He was about to make known who He is to a select group of people. The wedding attendees were about to see a miracle happen before their eyes and the Messiah stepped into His calling.

Jesus asked the workers to fill all the jugs with water. I can only imagine the snickering, whispering, and laughing only increased. I can imagine them laughing out loud and what He said. I can imagine many were confused, trying to understand why He would ask the workers to do this. Think of this in today's world. A stranger is at a wedding you are attending. He sees you with a bottle of soda, but the bottle is empty. You drank it all but want more. This stranger walks up to you and says go fill that bottle with water. I can probably guess you would look at him like he is crazy. You would wonder, why is he asking you to do this? Maybe even giggle thinking he is drunk. This is exactly what happened back then.

What were the followers thinking when they saw this miracle? Astonishment? Disbelief? After all, his time had not yet come. What did Mary think? Was it a sense of motherly pride for her son or was she astonished as well (or both)? Seeing what they saw, why didn't more people at least follow Him for a while to see what He was going to do next? They had to be curious. They had to wonder if this was the Messiah they had been expecting. Who was this Jesus from Nazareth? How could He do such a thing? How did Mary know He could do such a thing and it was time? So many questions and questions are good. This is awe and wonder. This is imagining what it would be like to be there when this happened and what they were thinking when they saw Jesus's first miracle. There are so many stories in the Bible and accounts not in the Bible of the miracles performed by Jesus. The awe and wonder of Jesus grew with every story.

There is the story about the Samaritan woman at the well. Jesus asked for a drink from the well in John 4.

***John 4-TPT*** [5] *Jesus arrived at the Samaritan village of Sychar, near the field that Jacob had given to his son Joseph.* [6-8] *Wearied by his long journey, he sat on the edge of Jacob's well, and sent his disciples into the village to buy food, for it was already afternoon. Soon a Samaritan woman came to draw water. Jesus said to her, "Give me a drink."*
[9] *She replied, "Why would a Jewish man ask a Samaritan woman for a drink of water?" (For Jews have no dealings with Samaritans.)*

*10* *Jesus replied, "If you only knew who I am and the gift that God wants to give you, you'd ask me for a drink, and I would give you living water."*

*11* *The woman replied, "But sir, you don't even have a bucket, and the well is very deep. So where do you find this 'living water'? 12 Do you really think that you are greater than our ancestor Jacob who dug this well and drank from it himself, along with his children and livestock?"*

*13* *Jesus answered, "If you drink from Jacob's well, you'll be thirsty again, 14 but if anyone drinks the living water I give them, they will never be thirsty again. For when you drink the water I give you, it becomes a gushing fountain of the Holy Spirit, flooding you with endless life!"*

*15* *The woman replied, "Let me drink that water so I'll never be thirsty again and won't have to come back here to draw water."*

*16* *Jesus said, "Go get your husband and bring him back here."*

*17* *"But I'm not married," the woman answered.*

*"That's true," Jesus said, 18 "for you've been married five times, and now you're living with a man who is not your husband. You have told the truth."*

*19* *The woman changed the subject. "You must be a prophet! 20 So tell me this: Why do our fathers worship God on this nearby mountain, but your people teach that Jerusalem is the place where we must worship. Who is right?"*

*Jesus responded, <sup>21</sup>* *"Believe me, dear woman, the time has come when you will worship the Father neither on a mountain nor in Jerusalem, but in your heart. <sup>22</sup> Your people don't really know the One they worship, but we Jews worship out of our experience, for it's from the Jews that salvation is available. <sup>23–24</sup> From now on, worshiping the Father will not be a matter of the right place but with a right heart. For God is a Spirit, and he longs to have sincere worshipers who adore him in the realm of the Spirit and in truth."*

*<sup>25</sup> The woman said, "This is all so confusing, but I do know that the Anointed One is coming—the true Messiah. And when he comes, he will tell us everything we need to know."*

*<sup>26</sup> Jesus said to her, "You don't have to wait any longer, the Anointed One is here speaking with you—I am the One you're looking for."*

*<sup>27</sup> At that moment, his disciples returned and were stunned to see Jesus speaking with a Samaritan woman, yet none of them dared ask him why or what they were discussing. <sup>28</sup> All at once, the woman left her water jar and ran off to her village and told everyone, <sup>29</sup> "Come and meet a man at the well who told me everything I've ever done! He could be the One we've been waiting for." <sup>30</sup> Hearing this, the people came streaming out of the village to go see Jesus.*

What an awesome story! Of all the people to reveal Himself and who He was first, He chose a Samaritan woman. A woman that had been with several men. A social outcast. She was not getting water in the morning with the other women. A woman that was married to one man and with another. A person with all kinds of issues. Why did He do that? Why did He choose her to reveal His glory to? Jesus must have saw something special in her. Isn't it amazing that Jesus sees what we can be and not just where we are at? What was the Samaritan woman thinking when she listened to Jesus proclaim He is the living water and that He is the Messiah they have been waiting for? Amazing! Simply incredible!

It is amazing that Jesus's words about living water touched her so immediately that her reply was I wanted that. His words pierced her so deeply that she knew she wanted the living water and wanted it now! The story doesn't end there. It wasn't just telling her she could have living water, but Jesus wanted to reveal Himself as the Messiah. Then Jesus told her to bring her husband so they can be together, knowing she is not with her husband. Then Jesus called her out about having multiple husbands and living in sin with another man. She told Jesus, "You must be a prophet." Then she asked Him a question. "Why do our fathers worship God on this nearby mountain, but your people teach that Jerusalem is the place where we must worship. Who is right?"

My awe and wonder moment was the Samaritan Woman. Why did she question Him? Did she think that when He was talking about the living water it wasn't Him? Was she testing Him? You have the Son of God, the Messiah, standing in front of you and you are concerned about the well? She truly did not understand who was in front of her nor did she understand what was about to happen. Jesus chose her, a Samaritan woman, a sinner, a person with a ton of issues to reveal who He is. Unreal. Why? Why her? What did Jesus see in her? How special would you feel going from social outcast to the one that will go down in history as the first person He revealed Himself as the Messiah to? This was an example of one of the many "sinners" that the Jewish leaders accused Jesus of hanging out with. In their eyes, she was not worthy. Jesus saw past her sins, her issues, her failures. He saw the exact person that He wanted to reveal who he was to. Simply incredible. Awe! Wonder!

## 4

## The healing in Bethesda & time to go fishing

Jesus had decided to return to Jerusalem to observe a Jewish feast. Here is where Jesus's compassion shows up.

***John 5- TPT** From Galilee, Jesus returned to Jerusalem to observe one of the Jewish feasts. ² Inside the city, near the Sheep Gate, there is a pool called in Aramaic, The House of Loving Kindness, surrounded by five covered porches. ³ Hundreds of sick people were lying under the covered porches—the paralyzed, the blind, and the crippled—all of them waiting for their healing. ⁴ For an angel of God periodically descended into the pool to stir the waters, and the first one who stepped into the pool after the waters swirled would instantly be healed.*

*⁵ Among the many sick people lying there was a man who had been disabled for thirty-eight years. ⁶ When Jesus saw him lying there, he knew that the man had been crippled for a long time. Jesus said to him, "Do you truly long to be well?"*

*⁷ The sick man answered, "Sir, there's no way I can get healed, for I have no one to lower me into the water when the angel comes. As soon as I try to crawl to the edge of the pool, someone else jumps in ahead of me."*

⁸ Jesus said to him, "Stand up! Pick up your sleeping mat and you will walk!" ⁹ Immediately he stood up—he was healed! So he rolled up his mat and walked again! Now Jesus worked this miracle on the Sabbath.

¹⁰ When the Jewish leaders saw the man walking along carrying his sleeping mat, they objected and said, "What are you doing carrying that? Don't you know it's the Sabbath? It's not lawful for you to carry things on the Sabbath!"

¹¹ He answered them, "The man who healed me told me to pick it up and walk."

¹² "What man?" they asked him. "Who was this man who ordered you to carry something on a Sabbath?" ¹³ But the healed man couldn't give them an answer, for he didn't yet know who it was, since Jesus had already slipped away into the crowd.

¹⁴ A short time later, Jesus found the man at the temple and said to him, "Look at you now! You're healed! Walk away from your sin so that nothing worse will happen to you."

¹⁵ Then the man went to the Jewish leaders to inform them, "It was Jesus who healed me!" ¹⁶ From that day forward the Jewish leaders began to persecute Jesus because of the things he did on the Sabbath.


Talk about being focused on the wrong things. Jesus healed someone that had been crippled for thirty-eight years and all they can talk about is the man breaking Jewish law? The man who for 38 years couldn't even carry a mat is now carrying one and they have a problem with it? Where was the celebration? I'm not saying there wasn't because there very well may have been, but not by the Jewish leaders. Even if they did not believe He was the Son of God, the Messiah, why would they not celebrate someone who was paralyzed for thirty-eight years? He wasn't tricking them. He was paralyzed for thirty-eight years. They knew he had been that way, but then came Jesus. Jesus's compassion. His healing. His power. His authority. His love. Jesus spoke a word and it was over.

What did that paralyzed man think when Jesus said, "Do you long to be well?" What did that paralyzed man think when Jesus asked him to stand up and walk? What did Jesus's followers think when they saw this miracle? Just another day at the office? I don't think so. The Bible says the former paralyzed man immediately stood up, rolled up his mat, and walked! What was going through that man's head after not walking, being paralyzed for thirty-eight years, all of a sudden walking? What was the hundreds of other sick, paralyzed, and blind people doing when this was done? You would think they would have been calling out to Him to heal them. Trying whatever they need to do to get His attention. I wonder, did Jesus heal the rest? Was the power of God so strong there at that minute that all of them were immediately healed? That is some great questions.

The Bible says the Jewish leaders were talking with the former paralyzed man about him carrying his mat on the Sabbath and how Jesus slipped away in the crowd. He did this as much as possible. He did not want attention on Him at that time.

Another interesting story in the Bible was when Jesus met Simon and Andrew.

***Matt 4- TPT*** *¹⁸ As he was walking by the shore of Lake Galilee, Jesus noticed two fishermen who were brothers. One was nicknamed Keefa (later called Peter), and the other was Andrew, his brother. Watching as they were casting their nets into the water, ¹⁹ Jesus called out to them and said, "Come and follow me, and I will transform you into men who catch people for God." ²⁰ Immediately they dropped their nets and left everything behind to follow Jesus. ²¹ Leaving there, Jesus found three other men sitting in a boat, mending their nets. Two were brothers, Jacob and John, and they were with their father, Zebedee. Jesus called Jacob and John to his side and said to them, "Come and follow me." ²² And at once they left their boat and their father, and began to follow Jesus.*

Fishermen. Why fishermen? At that time, the fishermen were not educated. They were not teachers of His word or the law. They were not preachers. They were poor fishermen. Hard workers, yes, but why would Jesus select them to be his followers, his disciples? What did He see in them? I have my theories but that is not what this book is about. There are questions throughout this book to inspire you to think. To wonder. To be in awe. Their lives were about to change. They were about to do something radical, crazy, and strange in the eyes of man. Stop doing what brings them income and food. Really? How crazy is that? A stranger they have never met walks up and says follow me and they do it. Crazy right?

I wonder, what was going through their minds when they saw this stranger? I am guessing they didn't immediately think he was the Messiah. When Jesus spoke though, it changed everything. They did not know exactly who He was, but they knew they had to find out. They saw and heard something different in Him. The words preceding out of Jesus's mouth were life to them. The words were powerful enough for them to drop what they were doing and follow Him. It's not like they were sitting on a beach or relaxing on a boat. This is what they did to support their family. Their income. Their food. Their ability to pay the very high Roman taxes. Their desire to find out more about this man was greater than their desire for money or food. The desire for the spiritual was greater than their desire for the natural.

After he had Peter and Andrew follow Him, He met Jacob and John, sons of Zebedee on another boat. Again, Jesus called for Jacob and John to drop everything and follow Him. They did. Amazing! Yet again, a stranger walked up to them and asked them to follow Him. Jesus spoke and they listened. They followed Him. They left their father on the boat to follow Him. Wait. What? What would Jewish leaders think of that? Would they say that John and Jacob were dishonoring their father by doing this? What did Zebedee think when he saw Jesus and heard Jesus speak to his sons to follow Him? Shock? Pride?

The destiny of those fishermen was greater than just fishing. Their lives were never the same. A major decision in their lives that would impact so many people was immediate. They did not question it. They did say, "why?" They didn't ask who he was. They didn't tell Jesus they would have to finish what they are doing first. They didn't tell Jesus He had the wrong guys. They weren't worthy of following Him (none of us are). They were just fishermen. Zero excuses, zero compromises, zero questions. They immediately dropped what they were doing and followed Him.

What was going through their minds when they did this? Did they second guess themselves in their own mind? What was Zebedee thinking when his sons followed Jesus and left him on that boat? Did they ask where they were going? Did they wonder how they would support their family, get food, shelter, clothing? Their faith was absolutely amazing! Their desire for the spiritual outweighed the desire for the natural. Their desire to learn more about this man outweighed their desire for money, food, shelter, or clothing.

They followed Him not because they knew He was the Son of God, the Messiah. Not at that time. They followed Him because they heard His words, saw Him, and knew they had to know more. This is a picture of how we should reach the lost. They hear our words, they see Jesus in us (actions and words), and they won't immediately know everything, but they will want to know more. What changed us? Who is that dwelling in us, walking with us, and radiating out of us?

The awe and wonder moment for me here is who Jesus used. He used fishermen. He didn't use Jewish spiritual leaders. He didn't even use teachers or community leaders. He chose ones that no person would choose for ministry. He chose what is viewed as the least among the people. No education. No proper teaching. They had passion. They had strength. They had a strong work ethic. Jesus saw the things in them that He wanted in leaders. In ministers. In the end, we all know the stories. The disciples (minus Judas) live their life following Jesus. Preaching about Jesus. Flowing in the power of Jesus. They died proclaiming how great Jesus is, how mighty he is, and how he defeated death, Hell, and the grave. Talk about living a life worthy of your calling!

## 5

## Sermon on the Mount & the Adulteress

The Sermon on the Mount was probably one of the biggest teaching sermons in history.

*Matt 5- TPT One day Jesus saw a vast crowd of people gathering to hear him, so he went up the slope of a hill and sat down. With his followers and disciples spread over the hillside, ² Jesus began to teach them:*

*³ "What happiness comes to you when you feel your spiritual poverty! For yours is the realm of heaven's kingdom.*

*⁴ "What delight comes to you when you wait upon the Lord! For you will find what you long for.*

*⁵ "What blessing comes to you when gentleness lives in you! For you will inherit the earth.*

*⁶ "How enriched you are when you crave righteousness! For you will be satisfied.*

*⁷ "How blessed you are when you demonstrate tender mercy! For tender mercy will be demonstrated to you.*

*⁸ "What bliss you experience when your heart is pure! For then your eyes will open to see more and more of God.*

*9* *"How joyful you are when you make peace! For then you will be recognized as a true child of God.*

*10* *"How enriched you are when persecuted for doing what is right! For then you experience the realm of heaven's kingdom.*

*11* *"How blessed you are when people insult and persecute you and speak all kinds of cruel lies about you because of your love for me!* *12* *So leap for joy—since your heavenly reward is great. For you are being rejected the same way the prophets were before you.*

*13* *"Your lives are like salt among the people. But if you, like salt, become bland, how can your 'saltiness' be restored? Flavorless salt is good for nothing and will be thrown out and trampled on by others.*

*14* *"Your lives light up the world. For how can you hide a city that stands on a hilltop?* *15* *And who would light a lamp and then hide it in an obscure place? Instead, it's placed where everyone in the house can benefit from its light.* *16* *So don't hide your light! Let it shine brightly before others, so that your commendable works will shine as light upon them, and then they will give their praise to your Father in heaven."*

*17* *"If you think I've come to set aside the law of Moses or the writings of the prophets, you're mistaken. I have come to bring to perfection all that has been written.* *18* *Indeed, I assure you, as long as heaven and earth endure, not even the smallest detail of the Law will be done away with until its purpose is complete.* *19* *So whoever violates even the least important of the commandments, and teaches others to do so, will be called least in heaven's kingdom. But whoever obeys them and teaches their truths to others will be called great in heaven's kingdom.* <sup>20</sup> *For I tell you, unless your lives are more pure and full of integrity than the religious scholars and the Pharisees, you will never enter heaven's kingdom."*

<sup>21</sup> *"You're familiar with the commandment taught to those of old: 'Do not murder or you will be judged.'* <sup>22</sup> *But I'm telling you, if you hold anger in your heart toward a fellow believer, you are subject to judgment. And whoever demeans and insults a fellow believer is answerable to the congregation. And whoever calls down curses upon a fellow believer is in danger of being sent to a fiery hell.*

<sup>23</sup> *"So then, if you are presenting a gift before the altar and suddenly you remember a quarrel you have with a fellow believer,* <sup>24</sup> *leave your gift there in front of the altar and go at once to apologize to the one who is offended. Then, after you have reconciled, come to the altar and present your gift.* <sup>25</sup> *It is always better to come to terms with the one who wants to sue you before you go to trial, or you may be found guilty by the judge, and he will hand you over to the officers, who will throw you into prison.* <sup>26</sup> *Believe me, you won't get out of prison until you have paid the full amount!"*

<sup>27</sup> *"Your ancestors have been taught, 'Never commit adultery.'* <sup>28</sup> *However, I say to you, if you look with lust in your eyes at a woman who is not your wife, you've already committed adultery in your heart.* <sup>29</sup> *If your right eye seduces you to fall into sin, then go blind in your right eye! For you're better off losing sight in one eye*

than to have your whole body thrown into hell. *30* And if your right hand entices you to sin, let it go limp and useless! For you're better off losing a part of your body than to have it all thrown into hell.

*31* "It has been said, 'Whoever divorces his wife must give her legal divorce papers.' *32* However, I say to you, if anyone divorces his wife for any reason, except for infidelity, he causes her to commit adultery, and whoever marries a divorced woman commits adultery."

*33* "Again, your ancestors were taught, 'Never swear an oath that you don't intend to keep, but keep your vows to the Lord God.' *34* However, I say to you, don't bind yourself by taking an oath at all. Don't swear by heaven, for heaven is where God's throne is placed. *35* Don't swear an oath by the earth, because it is the rug under God's feet, and not by Jerusalem, because it is the city of the Great King. *36* And why would you swear by your own head, because it's not in your power to turn a single hair white or black? But just let your words ring true. *37* A simple 'Yes' or 'No' will suffice. Anything beyond this springs from a deceiver.

*38* "Your ancestors have also been taught, 'Take an eye in exchange for an eye and a tooth in exchange for a tooth.' *39* However, I say to you, don't repay an evil act with another evil act. But whoever insults you by slapping you on the right cheek, turn the other to him as well. *40* If someone is determined to sue you for your coat, give him the shirt off your back as a gift in return. *41* And should people in authority take advantage of you, do more than what they *demand. ⁴² Learn to generously share what you have with those who ask for help, and don't close your heart to the one who comes to borrow from you."*

*⁴³ "Your ancestors have also been taught 'Love your neighbors and hate the one who hates you.' ⁴⁴ However, I say to you, love your enemy, bless the one who curses you, do something wonderful for the one who hates you, and respond to the very ones who persecute you by praying for them. ⁴⁵ For that will reveal your identity as children of your heavenly Father. He is kind to all by bringing the sunrise to warm and rainfall to refresh whether a person does what is good or evil. ⁴⁶ What reward do you deserve if you only love the loveable? Don't even the tax collectors do that? ⁴⁷ How are you any different from others if you limit your kindness only to your friends? Don't even the ungodly do that? ⁴⁸ Since you are children of a perfect Father in heaven, become perfect like him."*

The Sermon on the Mount by far is the longest teaching of Jesus's views of a Christian walk and to follow Him. Jesus wanted to change the thought process and poor teachings of the Jewish leaders, and to give them an idea of what should be. This was an explanation that we, as Christians, should live a noticeably different life than others. We should be a reflection of Jesus when people see us. In our actions, our attitudes, and our talk. We should strive to do better than the expectations of society. He set the record straight. His words were guidance on how to live, correct the mis-teachings, and the fulfillment of the Old Testament prophecy. There are at least 55 Old Testament Prophecies centering around Jesus and Jesus fulfilled them all.

I wonder, what were Jesus's followers thinking hearing this sermon? What were the Jewish Leaders thinking? I can imagine they were none too happy about His words. Jesus talked about being humble. Showing mercy. He said to have more integrity than the religious scholars and Pharisees. I imagine they were not happy. He was not saying that they had high integrity and ours were supposed to be higher. He was insinuating their appearance of high integrity but actually having low integrity. Their outside appearance, their appearance to others were most important to them.

The one thing that probably upset them the most was Jesus speaking with authority. He was speaking as if He has the authority to speak that way. He was speaking as if he had the authority to correct the law as taught by religious scholars and Jewish leaders. He spoke like He was the Son of God because He was and is! He was calling all believers to reconsider who God is and what it means to be a follower. The Sermon on the Mount gives us all guidance on how to live our daily lives, directly from the one with the authority to say so.

Then there was the adulteress. Talk about upsetting the Jewish leaders.

*John 8- **TPT** Jesus walked up the Mount of Olives near the city where he spent the night. ² Then at dawn Jesus appeared in the temple courts again, and soon all the people gathered around to listen to his words, so he sat down and taught them. ³ Then in the middle of his teaching, the religious scholars and the Pharisees broke through the crowd and brought a woman who had been caught in the act of committing adultery and made her stand in the middle of everyone.*

*⁴ Then they said to Jesus, "Teacher, we caught this woman in the very act of adultery. ⁵ Doesn't Moses' law command us to stone to death a woman like this? Tell us, what do you say we should do with her?" ⁶ They were only testing Jesus because they hoped to trap him with his own words and accuse him of breaking the laws of Moses.*

*But Jesus didn't answer them. Instead he simply bent down and wrote in the dust with his finger. ⁷ Angry, they kept insisting that he answer their question, so Jesus stood up and looked at them and said, "Let's have the man who has never had a sinful desire[f] throw the first stone at her." ⁸ And then he bent over again and wrote some more words in the dust.*

*⁹ Upon hearing that, her accusers slowly left the crowd one at a time, beginning with the oldest to the youngest, with a convicted conscience. [10] Until finally, Jesus was left alone with the woman still standing there in front of him. So he stood back up and said to her, "Dear woman, where are your accusers? Is there no one here to condemn you?"*

*[11] Looking around, she replied, "I see no one, Lord."*

*Jesus said, "Then I certainly don't condemn you either. Go, and from now on, be free from a life of sin."*

A truly awesome story. A story of corrupt leaders. A story of superiority complexes. A story of manipulation. A story of forgiveness. A story of setting the past teachings straight. These corrupt leaders tried and failed to trap Jesus into their teachings. The Law of Moses from their point of view. They knew that if they could show Jesus as a breaker of the Law of Moses in front of the crowd, they would leave and not follow Him. I wonder, what was going through her mind as she was being dragged to Jesus? I am guessing she was thinking she was going to die. Her sins had caught up with her and she was going to be stoned to death.

What were the Jewish leaders thinking while doing this? I am guessing they were thinking that now they have Him. Now they can show Jesus as a fake Messiah. After all, only a fake Messiah would call them out for their issues, right? Wrong. This Jesus cannot be the Messiah if He doesn't follow the Law of Moses as interpreted by them, can He? The Jewish leaders were so stuck in their traditions, in their interpretations of the law, they couldn't see what was really happening. The ironic thing is they knew the Old Testament prophecy of the coming Messiah but still could not see it. Why? If they were so well-educated, why couldn't they see who Jesus really was?

Was it a moment of opportunity when the woman was caught or was it planned ahead of time? They were so adamant about catching Jesus that they would do anything, in my opinion. I wonder, what was going through Jesus's mind when they asked Him that question? I imagine it was something to do with this. Are they really trying to catch me with this? Do they know who my Father is? Where do they think the Law of Moses came from? Was he naming all of the men who had been with this woman? Many probably were there when this was going on.

Jesus's compassion for people was simply amazing! He knew who she was and what she did. He could have said stone her. He could have thrown the first stone, even after his response as he was perfect. His actual response though was perfect. His response made them check themselves. Their sins, their issues, their desires. They looked in the mirror and recognized Jesus was right. They knew immediately. His words cut through them deep inside and convicted them. Their trap failed. I wonder, what were they thinking when Jesus gave His response? Did they feel like they had just been stabbed? Funny but a good analogy. What was the rest of the crowd thinking when they heard His response? Were they convicted as well? I imagine so.

After the conviction came forgiveness. Jesus told her she was forgiven of her sins. For the Jewish leaders, I can imagine that was a slap in the face after the conviction. This man (in their eyes) standing in front of a sinner giving her forgiveness. What or who gives Him the right to do this? Amazing! I think it is unreal to think about how many times we are in front of Jesus with our sins, our issues, our problems, and He says we are forgiven when we ask for forgiveness. What was going through the woman's mind when He said she was forgiven? Each time one of those rocks hit the ground was a sound of forgiveness. Forgiven. Forgiven. Forgiven.

My awe and wonder moment here was the story of the adulteress woman. This story was a reflection of Jesus's compassion and His love for us. He loves us so much he sees the good in us. He sees what we can be, not just who we are and what we have done. It was also a reflection of His authority. He was the only one on the Earth authorized to give forgiveness. The Jewish leaders would have been offended by that as well. When this happened, I imagine the Jewish leaders conspired even more to trap Jesus. Jesus could have condemned her. He could have pulled a political move and protected His own interests. He chose forgiveness. He chose love. He chose to protect and not condemn. Thank you Jesus for your choices that change lives, brought forgiveness, healing, and forgiveness.

## 6

## Jesus heals the paralyzed man & raises the dead

Healing was a huge part of Jesus's ministry. There are many records in and out of the Bible of Jesus's healings. One in particular, is in the Bible.

*Mark 2- TPT Several days later, Jesus returned to Capernaum, and the news quickly spread that he was back in town. ² Soon there were so many people crowded inside the house to hear him that there was no more room, even outside the door.*

*While Jesus was preaching the word of God, ³ four men arrived, carrying a paralyzed man. ⁴ But when they realized that they couldn't even get near him because of the crowd, they went up on top of the house and tore away the roof above Jesus' head. And when they had broken through, they lowered the paralyzed man on a stretcher right down in front of him! ⁵ When Jesus saw the extent of their faith, he said to the paralyzed man, "My son, your sins are now forgiven."*

*⁶ This offended some of the religious scholars who were present, and they reasoned among themselves, ⁷ "Who does he think he is to speak this way? This is blasphemy for sure! Only God himself can forgive sins!"*

*8 Jesus supernaturally perceived their thoughts and said to them, "Why are you being so skeptical? 9 Which is easier, to say to this paralyzed man, 'Your sins are now forgiven,' or, 'Stand up and walk!'?[a] 10 But to convince you that the Son of Man has been given authority to forgive sins, 11 I say to this man, 'Stand up, pick up your stretcher, and walk home.' " 12 Immediately the man was healed and sprang to his feet in front of everyone and left for home.*

*When the crowd witnessed this miracle, they were awestruck. They shouted praises to God and said, "We've never seen anything like this before!"*

Yet another amazing story of Jesus's power, authority, compassion, and love. Word spread quickly that Jesus was back in town. The crowds were growing with every healing, every forgiveness, every act of love. The people wanted to be around Him. To be close to Him. To hear him speak. To see Him. To see His glory and power. They needed Him. They wanted Him. The very Son of God, walking among them. The Holy One forgiving sins. The Anointed One delivering people. What would it be like to be right there with Jesus? To see all that He did. To see lives changed in an instant. People not walking most or all of their life all of a sudden are walking normal. Mind blown!

There were so many people at the house, inside and out, that the four men could not get the paralyzed man to Jesus. I can imagine that Jesus knew they were trying to get this man to Him. He could have walked out there to Him. He could have said make a path for them. Maybe Jesus wanted to see what they would do. To see someone so desperate for Him that they would do anything. They would climb the roof with a paralyzed man, tear through the roof, and lower him down to Jesus. That is desperation. This is faith. After all, why would they do all that if they weren't sure Jesus could and would heal him?

Of course, right as Jesus was performing this miracle, here comes the Jewish leaders. Jesus read their thoughts. He read their mail. Who does he think he is? Does he really think he can forgive sins? That is blasphemy. That is against God. Thoughts like that. I would flip that around. Who do they think they are? Do they think they are better than Jesus? Of course they do! They know more, they are smarter and wiser than Jesus. After all, he is from Nazareth. He was the son of a poor carpenter. He couldn't know more, could He? He couldn't heal, could He? He couldn't forgive sins, could He?

Jesus asked them which is easier: to forgive him of his sins or to rise up and walk? Almost like he was making a larger statement that they could do neither. The Jewish leaders walked around like they were the end all be all when it comes to anything religious. They walked around like they were above the ordinary man. Jesus once again angered them by doing what he was destined to do. To heal, restore, and deliver. The Bible says the former paralyzed man sprang to his feet. He leaped to his feet. It wasn't a soft, little, ok you should be able to walk at some point. It was immediate. He went from completely paralyzed to fully functioning in a split second. Unbelievable! Amazing! Awestruck! That's what the Bible says, they were awestruck, and they praised God! That is an awesome part of the story too. In the midst of a healing, in the midst of evil thoughts and doings, in the midst of unbelievers, people praised God. Don't you know the enemy was running away when the praises went up!

What do you think the former paralyzed man thought when he sprang up and walked? Was he thinking, is this temporary? What just happened? Is He the Messiah? I am pretty sure he didn't question where Jesus received His power. I imagine he had sheer and utter joy. What were the people in the crowd thinking? How amazing would it have been to see that? To know this person and to see Jesus do a miracle in him right in front of you? In the blink of an eye, this paralyzed man, who had to be carried in, leaped up and walked. Absolutely amazing!

Another incredible story is the story of Lazarus. He was the brother of Mary and Martha.

*John 11- TPT* *In the village of Bethany there was a man named Lazarus, and his sisters, Mary and Martha. Mary was the one who would anoint Jesus' feet with costly perfume and dry his feet with her long hair. One day Lazarus became very sick to the point of death.* *³ So his sisters sent a message to Jesus, "Lord, our brother Lazarus, the one you love, is very sick. Please come!"*

*⁴ When he heard this, he said, "This sickness will not end in death for Lazarus, but will bring glory and praise to God. This will reveal the greatness of the Son of God by what takes place."*

*⁵⁻⁶ Now even though Jesus loved Mary, Martha, and Lazarus, he remained where he was for two more days.* *⁷ Finally, on the third day, he said to his disciples, "Come. It's time to go to Bethany."*

*⁸ "But Teacher," they said to him, "do you really want to go back there? It was just a short time ago the people of Judea were going to stone you!"*

*⁹⁻¹⁰ Jesus replied, "Are there not twelve hours of daylight in every day? You can go through a day without the fear of stumbling when you walk in the One who gives light to the world. But you will stumble when the light is not in you, for you'll be walking in the dark."*

*¹¹ Then Jesus added, "Lazarus, our friend, has just fallen asleep. It's time that I go and awaken him."*

*¹² When they heard this, the disciples replied, "Lord, if he has just fallen asleep, then he'll get better."* *¹³ Jesus was speaking about*

*Lazarus' death, but the disciples presumed he was talking about natural sleep.*

*14 Then Jesus made it plain to them, "Lazarus is dead. 15 And for your sake, I'm glad I wasn't there, because now you have another opportunity to see who I am so that you will learn to trust in me. Come, let's go and see him."*

*16 So Thomas, nicknamed the Twin, remarked to the other disciples, "Let's go so that we can die with him."*

*17–18 Now when they arrived at Bethany, which was only about two miles from Jerusalem, Jesus found that Lazarus had already been in the tomb for four days. 19 Many friends of Mary and Martha had come from the region to console them over the loss of their brother. 20 And when Martha heard that Jesus was approaching the village, she went out to meet him, but Mary stayed in the house.*

*21 Martha said to Jesus, "My Lord, if only you had come sooner, my brother wouldn't have died. 22 But I know that if you were to ask God for anything, he would do it for you."*

*23 Jesus told her, "Your brother will rise and live."*

*24 She replied, "Yes, I know he will rise with everyone else on resurrection day."*

*25 "Martha," Jesus said, "You don't have to wait until then. I am the Resurrection, and I am Life Eternal. Anyone who clings to me in faith, even though he dies, will live forever. 26 And the one who lives by believing in me will never die. Do you believe this?"*

$^{27}$ Then Martha replied, "Yes, Lord, I do! I've always believed that you are the Anointed One, the Son of God who has come into the world for us!" $^{28}$ Then she left and hurried off to her sister, Mary, and called her aside from all the mourners and whispered to her, "The Master is here and he's asking for you."

$^{29}$ So when Mary heard this, she quickly went off to find him, $^{30}$ for Jesus was lingering outside the village at the same spot where Martha met him. $^{31}$ Now when Mary's friends who were comforting her noticed how quickly she ran out of the house, they followed her, assuming she was going to the tomb of her brother to mourn.

$^{32}$ When Mary finally found Jesus outside the village, she fell at his feet in tears and said, "Lord, if only you had been here, my brother would not have died."

$^{33}$ When Jesus looked at Mary and saw her weeping at his feet, and all her friends who were with her grieving, he shuddered with emotion and was deeply moved with tenderness and compassion. $^{34}$ He said to them, "Where did you bury him?"

"Lord, come with us and we'll show you," they replied.

$^{35}$ Then tears streamed down Jesus' face.

$^{36}$ Seeing Jesus weep caused many of the mourners to say, "Look how much he loved Lazarus." $^{37}$ Yet others said, "Isn't this the One who opens blind eyes? Why didn't he do something to keep Lazarus from dying?"

*38 Then Jesus, with intense emotions, came to the tomb—a cave with a stone placed over its entrance. 39 Jesus told them, "Roll away the stone."*

*Then Martha said, "But Lord, it's been four days since he died—by now his body is already decomposing!"*

*40 Jesus looked at her and said, "Didn't I tell you that if you will believe in me, you will see God unveil his power?"*

*41 So they rolled away the heavy stone. Jesus gazed into heaven and said, "Father, thank you that you have heard my prayer, 42 for you listen to every word I speak. Now, so that these who stand here with me will believe that you have sent me to the earth as your messenger, I will use the power you have given me." 43 Then with a loud voice Jesus shouted with authority: "Lazarus! Come out of the tomb!"*

*44 Then in front of everyone, Lazarus, who had died four days earlier, slowly hobbled out—he still had grave clothes tightly wrapped around his hands and feet and covering his face! Jesus said to them, "Unwrap him and let him loose."*

*45 From that day forward many of those who had come to visit Mary believed in him, for they had seen with their own eyes this amazing miracle! 46 But a few went back to inform the Pharisees about what Jesus had done.*

What a story! The first thing that sticks out here is Jesus could have healed him before he died. He could have healed him the moment he was told. He didn't have to travel there. He didn't have to wait for 4 days. Lazarus could have lived but how would Jesus show His resurrection power? There were always reasons for what He did. Things that we don't understand. This is where our faith and trust in Him lives. We trust that even if we don't understand or don't see what we think we should, we still trust in Him. Even though things don't happen the way we want, we still trust Him to do what is best for us.

Another thing that stood out was the followers of Jesus mentioned to Him how the people of Judea were ready to stone Jesus. It was dangerous for Him to return to Bethany, according to his followers. Jesus was not afraid. Jesus told his followers when you have the Anointed One in you, you do not fear. When Jesus said Lazarus was sleeping, can you imagine the giggles, the snickering, the laughter? Yeah, right. He's sleeping. How cruel. The family and friends mourning. Trying to get through their loss, this man says he is sleeping. After being dead for four days, then Jesus says it is time to go to Bethany.

Ironically, Mary, brother of Lazarus, told Jesus if he had been there, Lazarus would not have died. Her faith was strong enough to believe that Jesus could heal Lazarus but not enough to believe Jesus could raise him from the dead. *"When Jesus looked at Mary and saw her weeping at his feet, and all her friends who were with her grieving, he shuddered with emotion and was deeply moved with tenderness and compassion." John 11:33 TPT* Amazing! When Jesus saw Mary grieving at His feet, he shuddered with emotion and was deeply moved. His love for us, for His people are so great, his compassion was overwhelming. The emotions were so overwhelming that the Bible says Jesus cried.

Some said Jesus was weeping because he loved Lazarus so much. Some were still asking why he didn't come earlier so he could heal Lazarus. So, why was He crying? I have always wondered that too. Was it the sorrow, sympathy, and compassion felt for all mankind? He knew He was going to raise Lazarus from the dead so logic would be it wasn't because of that. This is more awe and wonder of Jesus. He cried. He cried over us. I will say that again, He cried over us! Our King cried over us. The King of Kings, the Lord of Lords, cares that much about us.

My awe and wonder moment for this chapter is, of course, Lazarus. What an amazing story! They pleaded with Jesus to come to heal him before he died. Then they complained that he was there after he died. They had enough faith to believe that Jesus could heal someone but not enough faith to believe Jesus could raise him from the dead. It had been four days. Lazarus was starting to stink. A dead body stench. The mourners thought that Jesus was mocking them. They couldn't be more wrong. Jesus was about to do something that no one could even imagine. Raise someone from the dead. I can imagine the pain and sorrow from the death of Lazarus. They were mourning his death. Then Jesus came on the scene.

Jesus, the only one who could do anything. The only one authorized to do anything, called Lazarus out. Out of his tomb. I could not even imagine the wild swing in emotions on that day. Their mourning turned to dancing. Their pain turned into celebration. Their sorrow turned into utter happiness. I could not even imagine the awestruck wonder of the crowd when Lazarus walked out of the tomb!

## 7

## Healings

A demon possessed man came to the synagogue where Jesus was teaching. We pick up the story in Mark 1.

***Mark 1 TPT*** *They went to Capernaum, and when the Sabbath came, Jesus went into the synagogue and began to teach.* ***22*** *The people were amazed at his teaching, because he taught them as one who had authority, not as the teachers of the law.* ***23*** *Just then a man in their synagogue who was possessed by an impure spirit cried out,* ***24*** *"What do you want with us, Jesus of Nazareth? Have you come to destroy us? I know who you are—the Holy One of God!"*

***25*** *"Be quiet!" said Jesus sternly. "Come out of him!"* ***26*** *The impure spirit shook the man violently and came out of him with a shriek.*

***27*** *The people were all so amazed that they asked each other, "What is this? A new teaching—and with authority! He even gives orders to impure spirits and they obey him."* ***28*** *News about him spread quickly over the whole region of Galilee.*

***29*** *As soon as they left the synagogue, they went with James and John to the home of Simon and Andrew.* ***30*** *Simon's mother-in-law* *was in bed with a fever, and they immediately told Jesus about her. 31 So he went to her, took her hand and helped her up. The fever left her and she began to wait on them.*

*32 That evening after sunset the people brought to Jesus all the sick and demon-possessed. 33 The whole town gathered at the door, 34 and Jesus healed many who had various diseases. He also drove out many demons, but he would not let the demons speak because they knew who he was.*

You know the old saying, even the devil comes to church, right? The demon was there, in the synagogue where Jesus was teaching. I wonder, what were the people attending thinking when they heard Jesus speak in person? The Bible said they were amazed. Just amazed or was it more? No one had ever taught like this before. It wasn't law teaching as they are used to. Jesus spoke with authority. He spoke with wisdom, love, compassion, but correcting the improper teachings of the Jewish leaders. I am in awe that they accepted His words and accepted them instead of saying He was speaking blasphemy. They were drawn to His teaching. I can imagine their eyes were glued on Him, our beautiful Savior.

Then, right in the middle of Jesus' teaching. Right in the middle of Jesus speaking about the wonders of God, the power of God, the holiness of God, here comes the enemy. Right on time.

The demon possessed man cried out asking what Jesus wants with them. Then they proclaimed Him as the Holy one of God. I wonder, what was the man doing there? Did he come to his own decision? Was he brought by others? Did the demon get him to go? It is awesome that even demons know who Jesus is. Amazing! Even the demons proclaim that Jesus is the Holy One. I wonder, if the Jewish leaders didn't believe their eyes seeing all that Jesus did, they didn't believe Jesus's words, they didn't believe others saying who He was, and they don't believe a demon, were they ever going to believe that Jesus was the Messiah?

Jesus told the demon to be quiet. He silenced him. He had and used the authority to shut the enemy up. The Bible says the man shook and the demon fled. The demon had to flee with Jesus's words. What power! What authority! The awe and wonder of Jesus. Who knows how long that demon had been there? How long that man had struggled with that demon being there. I can imagine that man having to deal with that demon, day after day. In one instance, one second, one moment, Jesus stepped on the scene. Jesus spoke a word and changed that man's life, forever! When Jesus steps on the scene, our lives are never the same. We should not worship the same. We should not love the same. He deserves all our worship, all our praise, all our love.

Another amazing story of the awe and wonder of Jesus is the story of Jesus healing the leper in Mark 1.

*Mark 1- TPT* *40 A man with leprosy came to him and begged him on his knees, "If you are willing, you can make me clean."*

*41 Jesus was indignant. He reached out his hand and touched the man. "I am willing," he said. "Be clean!" 42 Immediately the leprosy left him and he was cleansed.*

*43 Jesus sent him away at once with a strong warning: 44 "See that you don't tell this to anyone. But go, show yourself to the priest and offer the sacrifices that Moses commanded for your cleansing, as a testimony to them." 45 Instead he went out and began to talk freely, spreading the news. As a result, Jesus could no longer enter a town openly but stayed outside in lonely places. Yet the people still came to him from everywhere.*

How amazing would it be to see the scene that unfolded there. The man with leprosy, begging Jesus, on his knees. Begging to be healed. Begging. How desperate would a person have to be to beg Jesus for healing? Crying out to the living God in front of everyone. Embarrassing? Probably. Taking a chance? Absolutely. Jesus could have turned him away, although we know he would not. Crazy? In some people's eyes, definitely. We all know what Jesus was going to do. Jesus's love kicks in. His compassion kicks in. His authority kicks in. He touches the unclean and performs the miracle he was waiting for. The healing he was wanting more than anything. More than any embarrassment. More than worrying about what others were thinking. More than anything. He was going after his healing. Going after his miracle. He had a date with destiny, and he was not going to let anything stop him!

*Luke 7- TPT* *After Jesus finished giving revelation to the people on the hillside, he went on to Capernaum. 2–3 A Roman military captain there had a beloved servant whom he valued highly, and who was sick to the point of death. When the captain heard that Jesus was in the city, he sent some respected Jewish elders to plead with him to come and heal his dying servant. 4 So they came to Jesus and told him, "The Roman captain is a wonderful man. If anyone deserves a visit from you, it is him. Won't you please come to his home and heal his servant? 5 For he loves the Jewish people, and he even built our meeting hall for us."*

*6–7 Jesus started off with them, but on his way there, friends of the captain stopped him and delivered this message: "Master, don't bother to come to me in person, for I am not good enough for you to enter my home. I'm not worthy enough to even come out to meet one like you. But if you would just speak the word of healing from right where you are, I know that my servant will be healed.*

*8 I am an ordinary man. Yet I understand the power of authority, and I see that authority operating through you. I have soldiers under me who obey everything I command. I also have authorities over me whom I likewise obey. So Master, just speak the word and healing will flow."*

*9 Jesus marveled at this. He turned around and said to the crowd who had followed him, "Listen, everyone! Never have I found among the people of God a man like this who believes so strongly in me." 10 Jesus then spoke the healing word from a distance. When the man's friends returned to the home, they found the servant completely healed and doing fine.*

A Roman Soldier came to Jesus. A Roman. A Roman Soldier. A Roman Captain. Coming to a Jew. Unreal. In Roman culture, the Jews were trash to them. Less of a person to them. Although the Bible says this particular Roman liked Jews, I can imagine that if any of the Roman executives over the Roman Captain would have heard or saw him asking for a Jew's help, they would have probably killed him. A Roman coming to a Jew for help. That would have not happened under nearly any circumstance. This was different though. There was someone there that was different. Jesus, the Messiah, the Healer, The Anointed One, was there.

The Roman Soldier's beloved servant was sick near death. He sent some well-respected Jewish leaders to bring Jesus to his home to heal the servant. On His way there, friends of the Roman Captain delivered a message to Jesus. *"Master, don't bother to come to me in person, for I am not good enough for you to enter my home. I'm not worthy enough to even come out to meet one like you. But if you would just speak the word of healing from right where you are, I know that my servant will be healed. [8] I am an ordinary man. Yet I understand the power of authority, and I see that authority operating through you. I have soldiers under me who obey everything I command. I also have authorities over me whom I likewise obey. So Master, just speak the word and healing will flow."*

What a powerful statement! You should read that statement over. A Roman Soldier said this! Absolutely amazing!! First off, a Roman Captain called a Jew, Master. Then showing his humbleness by stating he is not worthy for Jesus to enter his home. A Roman saying he is not worthy for a Jew to enter his home. Really? Then he speaks the very powerful words reflecting Jesus's power and authority. He told Jesus to just speak the word of healing from where he was at and his servant would be healed. Wow! His level of faith was amazing! Then he said, healing will flow. Healing will flow! A Roman Soldier said healing will flow! Astonishing!

I want to see that! I want to see a time come where healing flows!! Flowing like a river. The blind sees, the deaf hear, the crippled walk. cancer disappears, the dead raised, sickness gone, disease gone! How I long to see Jesus's name be lifted high on the Earth for this! After all, Jesus is the only one authorized. He is the only one able!! He is the One and only One! Only the creator can re-create. What he took, the blood he shed, wasn't for nothing. He took those stripes on his back for healing. It was a level of pain we couldn't even imagine. Our King did this for us! He did it for you! He did it for me!

Then comes the story of the widow woman. Another marvelous story of Jesus's love and compassion for His people.

*Luke 7- TPT* [11] *Shortly afterward, Jesus left on a journey to the village of Nain, with a massive crowd of people following him, and his disciples.* [12] *As he approached the village, he met a multitude of people in a funeral procession, who were mourning as they carried the body of a young man to the cemetery. The boy was his mother's only son, and she was a widow.* [13] *When the Lord saw the grieving mother, his heart broke for her. With great tenderness he said to her, "Please don't cry."* [14] *Then he stepped up to the coffin and touched it. When the pallbearers came to a halt, Jesus spoke directly to the corpse, "Young man, I say to you, arise and live!"*

*15 Immediately, the young man moved, sat up, and spoke to those nearby. Jesus presented the son to his mother, alive! 16 A tremendous sense of holy mystery swept over the crowd. They shouted praises to God, saying, "God himself has blessed us by visiting his people! A great prophet has appeared among us!" 17 The news of Jesus and this miracle raced throughout Judea and the entire surrounding region.*

What an amazing turn of events for the widow woman. She already had experienced death. She was a widow. The pain, the agony of losing your mate and now her only son. I could not even imagine the pain, the hurt, the anguish, the emptiness inside her, the unbelievable grief. Then Jesus. Then came Jesus. The Holy One. Jesus spoke 9 simple but ultimately powerful words to the corpse. "Young man, I say to you, arise and live!" Can you imagine seeing that happen? Can you imagine what the people in the funeral procession were thinking? Such as a somber moment. The grief of a child that died. The crying, the pain, the hurt. All of that ended when Jesus came on the scene.

I can imagine the shock that someone would stop a funeral procession then start speaking to the corpse. What would you think if this happened to you? I would be in total shock! It would be amazing to see what actually transpired though, on that day. There is a common theme throughout the Bible with Jesus and His healings. Compassion and love. Jesus had compassion for the woman. The compassion and love for His people is incredible. What an awesome sight to be able to see that! The dead rising, alive and well. The awe and wonder of that story is absolutely amazing. It was absolutely beautiful. Jesus turning misery into celebration. Mourning into dancing. Pain into happiness.

Then there was the story of the paralyzed man. This is an amazing story of Jesus's compassion.

*John 5- TPT. 5 From Galilee, Jesus returned to Jerusalem to observe one of the Jewish feasts. 2 Inside the city, near the Sheep Gate, there is a pool called in Aramaic, The House of Loving Kindness, surrounded by five covered porches. 3 Hundreds of sick people were lying under the covered porches—the paralyzed, the blind, and the crippled—all of them waiting for their healing. 4 For an angel of God periodically descended into the pool to stir the waters, and the first one who stepped into the pool after the waters swirled would instantly be healed.*

*5 Among the many sick people lying there was a man who had been disabled for thirty-eight years. 6 When Jesus saw him lying there, he knew that the man had been crippled for a long time. Jesus said to him, "Do you truly long to be well?"*

*7 The sick man answered, "Sir, there's no way I can get healed, for I have no one to lower me into the water when the angel comes. As soon as I try to crawl to the edge of the pool, someone else jumps in ahead of me."*

*8 Jesus said to him, "Stand up! Pick up your sleeping mat and you will walk!" 9 Immediately he stood up—he was healed! So he rolled up his mat and walked again! Now Jesus worked this miracle on the Sabbath.*

*10 When the Jewish leaders saw the man walking along carrying his sleeping mat, they objected and said, "What are you doing carrying that? Don't you know it's the Sabbath? It's not lawful for you to carry things on the Sabbath!"*

*11 He answered them, "The man who healed me told me to pick it up and walk."*

*12 "What man?" they asked him. "Who was this man who ordered you to carry something on a Sabbath?" 13 But the healed man couldn't give them an answer, for he didn't yet know who it was, since Jesus had already slipped away into the crowd.*

14 A short time later, Jesus found the man at the temple and said to him, "Look at you now! You're healed! Walk away from your sin so that nothing worse will happen to you."

15 Then the man went to the Jewish leaders to inform them, "It was Jesus who healed me!" 16 From that day forward the Jewish leaders began to persecute Jesus because of the things he did on the Sabbath.

17 Jesus answered his critics by saying, "Every day my Father is at work, and I will be, too!" 18 This infuriated them and made them all the more eager to devise a plan to kill him. For not only did he break their Sabbath rules, but he also called God "my Father," which made him equal to God.

19 So Jesus said, "I speak to you eternal truth. The Son is unable to do anything from himself or through his own initiative. I only do the works that I see the Father doing, for the Son does the same works as his Father.

20 "Because the Father loves his Son so much, he always reveals to him everything that he is about to do. And you will all be amazed when he shows him even greater works than what you've seen so far! 21 For just as the Father has power to raise the dead, the Son will also raise the dead and give life to whomever he wants.

*22 "The Father judges no one, for he has given to the Son all the authority to judge. 23 Therefore, the honor that belongs to the Father he will now share with his Son. So if you refuse to honor the Son, you are refusing to honor the Father who sent him.*

*24 "I speak to you an eternal truth: if you embrace my message and believe in the One who sent me, you will never face condemnation. In me, you have already passed from the realm of death into eternal life!"*

The first thing that stands out to me is thirty-eight years. Thirty-eight years! He was paralyzed for 38 years. How much did his muscles deteriorate after 38 years? How frustrating was it to be at that pool for years, maybe even decades, to not be the one who gets healed? The one who got to where the waters were stirred first. People climbing over you. Knocking you over. Shoving you down. Getting their healing. Walking away healed. You are left there, paralyzed, tired, hurting, and no hope. But Jesus. The provider of hope. The Master of healing. Jesus showed up on the scene. Jesus was about to change a man's life forever. He was about to set this man on a new road. A road paved with healing, with hope, with celebration, and with him walking!

The next thing is Jesus asked him, "Do you truly long to be well?" The man explained to Jesus why he couldn't get to the place where the waters were stirred first. I find it amazing that the one person that could heal him was standing right in front of him and all he was talking about is why he couldn't get his healing. At that moment, he did not even realize his life was about to change dramatically. What was Jesus thinking at that moment? Compassion? Absolutely. Love? Of course. How about the people around him? What were they thinking, seeing this miracle happen before their eyes? Seeing a person's entire future be changed in an instant. Seeing a person who has not walked in thirty-eight years suddenly stand up, roll-up his mat, and walk. What a moment of awe. What a moment to marvel at the compassion, the love, and the power of Jesus, right in front of them.

Naturally, one must think, how did he walk? He had not walked in thirty-eight years. His muscles had to be depleted. His bones brittle. There is no way someone could just stand up and walk instantly. Except with Jesus. Jesus not only healed him of his condition, but he also restored his muscles, his bones, his balance, his whole ability to walk. Instantly that man stood up and walked. Instantly. He didn't go through rehab. He didn't get a rehab specialist to go through exercises to strengthen his body. His healing was more than just a healing. It was a complete transformation.

What is amazing is being able to have this happen, to see a man who has not walked in thirty-eight years be healed and the one thing they focus on is Jesus healing on the Sabbath. Really? That man's life is changed forever by Jesus, walking, running, leaping, jumping, and more and they are concerned about when he healed him? Every prophecy in the Old Testament has come alive right in front of them and they are concerned about such a minor issue in comparison to this man's paralysis? All of that man's tears. All of his anguish. All of his hopelessness. The most vulnerable of people needing Jesus. I couldn't even imagine what he went through. Thirty-eight years' worth. Day after day. Month after month. Year after year. That is a level of hopelessness that only a handful of people could understand.

I find it amazing that he would not give up. He could have just given up and said this is how it's going to be. I am just not going to walk again. I am just going to live this way forever, but he did not. I'm sure he had days when he wanted to give up. Days where the hopelessness was greater. The fear. The desperation. He was basically left for dead. Jesus is the one, the only one, that could raise him. Heal him. Change his life. A thirty-eight-year story waiting for a miracle. How could anyone not be absolutely bawling after seeing that? I admit, I would be crying tears of joy! Joy for the former paralyzed man and joy for the fact that the Messiah is here. The

Great Healer is here. El Shaddai is here. Yeshua is here. The Son of Man is here.

My Awe and Wonder moment is that exact moment. I am awestruck thinking about that moment. Someone that went through so much. Struggling to survive. Not being able to walk. Mobility at that time for people that could not walk was nil. But Jesus. The Great Healer. The I am that I am. The Powerful One. His compassion, His love for His people was so great that He had to step in. He said to say enough is enough for this man. Once it happened, this man became a walking, talking testimony of Jesus's power, His authority, His love, and His compassion for all of us.

## 8

## Calming the waters and here piggy piggy

Jesus did some other miracles that were against everything man has ever seen,

*Luke 8- TPT* [26-29] *As soon as they stepped ashore on the eastern side of the lake in the land of the Gerasenes, the disciples were confronted by a demon-possessed madman from a nearby town. Many times he had been put under guard and bound with chains, but the many demons inside him had repeatedly thrown him into convulsions, breaking his shackles and driving him out of the town into the countryside. He had been demonized for a long time and was living naked in a cemetery among the tombs. When he saw Jesus, he fell at his feet and screamed out, "What are you doing here? You are Jesus, the Son of the Most High God!"*
*Jesus commanded the demons to come out of him, and they shouted, "We beg you, don't torture us!"*

[30] *Jesus asked the man, "What is your name?"*

"Mob," the demons answered. "We are a mob, for there are many of us here in this man. <sup>31</sup> We beg you, don't banish us into the Abyss!"

<sup>32</sup> On the hillside nearby, there was a large herd of pigs, and the demons pleaded with Jesus, "Let us enter into the pigs." <sup>33</sup> So Jesus ordered all the "mob" of demons to come out of the man and enter the pigs. The crazed herd of swine stampeded over the cliff into the lake and all of them drowned.

<sup>34</sup> When the herders tending the pigs saw what had happened, they ran off in fear and reported it to the nearby town and throughout the countryside. <sup>35</sup> Then the people of the region came out to see for themselves what had happened. When they came to where Jesus was, they discovered the notorious madman totally set free. He was clothed, speaking intelligently, and sitting at the feet of Jesus. They were shocked! <sup>36</sup> Then eyewitnesses to the miracle reported all that they had seen and how Jesus completely delivered the demonized man from his torment.

After hearing about such amazing power, the townspeople became frightened. <sup>37</sup> Soon all the people of the region of the Gerasenes and the surrounding country pleaded with Jesus to leave them, for they were gripped with fear. So Jesus got into the boat, intending to return to Galilee. <sup>38</sup> But the man who had been set free begged Jesus over and over not to leave, saying, "Let me be with you!"

*Jesus sent him away with these instructions:* [39] *"Return to your home and your family, and tell them all the wonderful things God has done for you." So the man went back and preached to everyone who would listen about the amazing miracle Jesus had worked in his life.*

[40] *When Jesus returned to Galilee, the crowds were overjoyed, for they had been waiting for him to arrive.* [41-42] *Just then, a man named Jairus, the leader of the local Jewish congregation, fell before Jesus' feet. He desperately begged him to come and heal his twelve-year-old daughter, his only child, because she was at the point of death.*

*As Jesus started to go with him to his home to see her, a large crowd surrounded him.* [43] *In the crowd that day was a woman who had suffered greatly for twelve years from slow bleeding. Even though she had spent all that she had on healers, she was still suffering.* [44] *Pressing in through the crowd, she came up behind Jesus and touched the fringe of his garment. Instantly her bleeding stopped and she was healed.*

[45] *Jesus suddenly stopped and said to his disciples, "Someone touched me. Who was it?"*

*While they all denied it, Peter pointed out, "Master, everyone is touching you, trying to get close to you. The crowds are so thick we can't walk through all these people without being jostled."*

[46] Jesus replied, "Yes, but I felt power surge through me. Someone touched me to be healed, and they received their healing."

[47] When the woman realized she couldn't hide any longer, she came and fell trembling at Jesus' feet. Before the entire crowd she declared, "I was desperate to touch you, Jesus, for I knew if I could just touch even the fringe of your garment I would be healed."

[48] Jesus responded, "Beloved daughter, your faith in me released your healing. You may go with my peace."

[49] While Jesus was still speaking to the woman, someone came from Jairus' house and told him, "There's no need to bother the Master any further. Your daughter has passed away. She's gone."

[50] When Jesus heard this, he turned to Jairus and said, "Don't yield to your fear. Have faith in me and she will live again."

[51] When they arrived at the house, Jesus allowed only Peter, John, and Jacob—along with the child's parents—to go inside. [52] Jesus told those left outside, who were sobbing and wailing with grief, "Stop crying. She is not dead; she's just asleep and must be awakened."

[53] They laughed at him, knowing for certain that she had died.

[54] Jesus approached the body, took the girl by her hand, and called out with a loud voice, "My sleeping child, awake! Rise up!"

*55-56 Instantly her spirit returned to her body and she stood up.*

*Jesus directed her stunned parents to give her something to eat and ordered them to tell no one what just happened.*

A couple of awe-inspiring stories. So much to go through here. Let's start with the demonized man. Demonized. In some people's view, absolutely crazy. Many times, he was bound by shackles to try to control him. Those shackles were broken by the demons. Demons, plural. Not just one but a mob. In some translations, they used the word Legions. In Biblical times, a Roman Legion numbered 6000. If that was the case here, it was many legions or many times 6000. That many demons in one man. That's kind of scary movie stuff on steroids.

This broke the man into convulsions, breaking his shackles, and driving him out of town into the countryside. He was demonized for a long time, living at a cemetery. He was naked. He was consumed with demons. Total despair. Total hopelessness. He lost everything. He was living, sort of living, among the dead. Alone. Afraid. Naked. No one would come near him, until one day someone did. Jesus. The Living Hope. The very Son of God. Jesus walked onto the scene and was recognized immediately.

The demons said, "What are you doing here? You are Jesus, the Son of the Most High God." Ironically legions of demons could recognize Him but Jewish Leaders, Priests, and more could not. The demons were scared. The Son of the Most High God is there. They knew it was over! They begged Jesus. Begged. I'm sorry but I think that is kind of funny. In seconds, they begged Jesus for mercy while torturing the man for a long time. They asked to be sent into the pigs instead of being sent into the abyss. Jesus did as they asked and commanded them to go into the pigs. The pigs ran off the cliff and drowned. Talk about being careful what you ask for.

The townspeople discovered the *notorious* madman totally set free. He was clothed, speaking intelligently, and sitting at the feet of Jesus. They were shocked! One would think they would worship Jesus. Celebrate the man's deliverance. Be happy that the Messiah was there. They were not. They were in fear. As a matter of fact, the Bible says they were gripped with fear. Fear controlled them. They pleaded for Jesus to leave. They pleaded for JESUS to leave! The one that delivered that man. The Holy One. The one that had compassion for the man and helped him was asked to leave. They let fear become greater in them than the Messiah that was right in front of them. The delivered man asked Jesus to stay. He wanted to be with Him. Jesus told him to go to his family and tell everyone what God had done for him.

Then Jesus returned to Galilee to "crowds." Crowds of people waiting on Jesus. They were overjoyed. The Messiah was there! The crowds were desperate to see Him. One, however, was desperate to more than just see him. Jairus, leader of a local Jewish congregation. He fell before Jesus's feet. Can you imagine the scene? Being able to fall at Jesus's feet. My Lord and My God. Being able to be at Jesus's feet even for a second would be beyond words. Jairus was there for more than worship though. He was not there as a Jewish leader, a Galilean, a Jew, or even a man. He was there as a Father. A parent. His little girl was sick to the point of death. I have never been to that point as a parent, thank God. I could not even imagine what he was going though. His only child. His little girl.

On the way there, Jesus was about to meet a woman of amazing faith. This woman had suffered twelve years with an issue of blood. She spent all her money trying to get healed. Nothing. I can imagine the frustration. Trying anything and everything to get well. The questions. The depression. The hopelessness. Wondering why her? Wondering why she is having this issue. Then desperation comes. Then Jesus comes. She would not be denied. The crowds would not stop her. Her own doubt would not stop her. She knew Jesus was the answer.

She pressed through the crowd. The crowd was thick with people. The crowd was so thick that they could not help being bumped up against each other. She continued to press. She came up behind Jesus and touched the hem of His garment. Instantly. The Bible says instantly the blood stopped and she was healed. Instantly. Think about that word. Instantly. Immediately the blood stopped and she was healed. What did she think when that happened? What was going through her mind when the very power of God was flowing through her? In an instant, her life was changed. In an instant, her healing came to her. In an instant, the only thing she has wanted for the last 12 years came to fruition.

Jesus suddenly stopped and asked who touched him. Kind of funny considering he was being touched by, well, everyone. This was different though. His power surged through Him. What did you think that looked like? The power of God surging through Him. Could you imagine Jesus standing there with the power of God surging through Him? Awesome! Then Jesus said some powerful words, "Someone touched me to be healed, and they received their healing." Jesus did not have to look. Up to that point in the story, He heard no one step up and say they touched him. Yet Jesus stated that the person that touched Him received their healing. How powerful! How amazing! To see that woman be healed right in front of your eyes.

The woman could hide no longer. She spoke out and said she was the one and fell, trembling at Jesus's feet. She was so desperate for her healing she fought through the crowd to get it. She swallowed her pride and went for it. Her desperation was greater than her fear. She was at the feet of Jesus, the Healer. The Master. The Anointed One. The Great I am. She told him she knew that if she could just touch the hem of his garment, she would be healed. What an awesome level of faith! What do you think it was like, touching the hem of Jesus's garment? The power of God surging through you. What do you think it was like being that close to Jesus? Hanging on every word. Awestruck by the miracles. Joyous knowing the Messiah you had been waiting for was there. That part of the story ends with Jesus saying her faith in Him released her healing. Another amazingly powerful statement!

While Jesus was speaking with the woman, a man came up to them to tell them that Jairus's daughter had passed away. There was no need to bring Jesus to his home. No need to "bother" him anymore. I find that funny. Jesus's compassion for His people is too great to think he is being bothered by asking Him to heal a sick child. Also, why would they not think that Jesus could raise her from the dead as He did others? Jesus spoke to Jairus telling him not to give into fear. He said for Jairus to believe in Him. To have faith.

He arrived seeing weeping people. Grieving people. He told them she was not dead but sleeping. They laughed at him. They were positive she was dead, and they were correct. However, they didn't take into consideration who just arrived on the scene. The very person that can raise her, heal her, and take away all of the family's grief was there. He was being mocked though. Laughed at. Treating him like He was crazy. While I don't understand why anyone would treat Jesus this way, they were.

Jesus took a couple of disciples in with him along with the parents. He called out loudly for her to wake up. Instantly. There is that word again. Instantly. Immediately her spirit entered her body again and she stood up. What was that like? What did that look like? She was dead, then she stood up, alive. What did she see while she was dead? What did it feel like all of a sudden being alive again? Standing up, looking at the face of Jesus. What were her parents thinking seeing this? I am sure they wanted to hope. They wanted to believe in the impossible. I am sure every parent that has gone through the death of a child has those thoughts.

Did they fall down and worship Jesus after witnessing this miracle? Did they shout for joy as the Messiah is among them? What was their level of awe seeing this? I can imagine it had to be off the charts. The parents had to be experiencing a ton of different emotions going from unspeakable grief, pain, misery, anguish to skepticism, cautious hope, to disbelief, awe, wonder, joy, elation, and so many more. Jesus truly turned their mourning into dancing!

The awe and wonder moment for me here is the woman with the issue of blood. She said enough is enough. She wasn't going to take it anymore. Her healing was just a few feet from her. She barreled through people. She pushed through the doubt. Through the fear. Through the past disappointments. Through the mocking. Through the negativity. She was not going to be denied. She decided she was going to get her healing from the only one who could give it to her. She didn't ask Jesus to heal her. Her faith was stronger than simply asking. She knew that all she had to do was touch the hem of his garment and she would be healed. Awesome!

## 9

## Food and water

There were also some great stories of non-healing miracles with Jesus with some healings sprinkled in.

*Mark 6- TPT* *30 The apostles returned from their mission and gathered around Jesus and told him everything they had done and taught.*

*31 There was such a swirl of activity around Jesus, with so many people coming and going, that they were unable to even eat a meal. So Jesus said to his disciples, "Come, let's take a break and find a secluded place where you can rest a while." 32 They slipped away and left by sailboat for a deserted spot. 33 But many of the people saw them leaving and realized where they were headed, so they took off running along the shore. Then people from the surrounding towns joined them in the chase, and a large crowd got there ahead of them.*

*34 By the time Jesus came ashore, a massive crowd was waiting. At the sight of them, his heart was filled with compassion, because they seemed like wandering sheep who had no shepherd. So he taught them many wonderful things.*

*35 Late that afternoon, his disciples said, "It's getting really late and we're here in this remote place with nothing to eat. 36 You should send the crowds away so they can go into the surrounding villages and buy food."*

*37 But he answered them, "You give them something to eat."*

*"Are you sure?" they replied. "You really want us to go buy them supper? It would cost a small fortune to feed all these thousands of hungry people."*

*38 "How many loaves of bread do you have?" he asked. "Go and see." After they had looked around, they came back and said, "Five—plus a couple of fish."*

*39 Then he instructed them to organize the crowd and have them sit down in groups on the grass. 40 So they had them sit down in groups of hundreds and fifties. 41 Then Jesus took the five loaves and two fish, gazed into heaven, and gave thanks to God. He broke the bread and the two fish and distributed them to his disciples to serve the people—and the food was multiplied in front of their eyes! 42 Everyone had plenty to eat and was fully satisfied. 43 Then the twelve disciples picked up what remained, and each of them ended up with a basket full of leftovers! 44 Altogether, five thousand families were fed that day!*

*45 After everyone had their meal, Jesus instructed his disciples to get back into the boat and go on ahead of him and sail to the other side to Bethsaida. ⁴⁶ So he dispersed the crowd, said good-bye to his disciples, then slipped away to pray on the mountain.*

*⁴⁷ As night fell, the boat was in the middle of the lake and Jesus was alone on land. ⁴⁸ The wind was against the disciples and he could see that they were straining at the oars, trying to make headway.*

*When it was almost morning, Jesus came to them, walking on the surface of the water, and he started to pass by them. ⁴⁹⁻⁵⁰ When they all saw him walking on the waves, they thought he was a ghost and screamed out in terror. But he said to them at once, "Don't yield to fear. Have courage. It's really me—I Am!"*

*⁵¹ Then he came closer and climbed into the boat with them, and immediately the stormy wind became still. They were completely and utterly overwhelmed with astonishment. ⁵² Their doubting hearts had not grasped his authority and power over all things in spite of just having witnessed the miraculous feeding.*

*⁵³ They made landfall at Gennesaret and anchored there. ⁵⁴ The moment they got out of the boat, everyone recognized that it was Jesus, the healer! ⁵⁵ So they ran throughout the region, telling the people, "Bring all the sick—even those too sick to walk and bring them on mats!" ⁵⁶ Wherever he went, in the countryside, villages, or towns, they placed the sick on mats in the streets or in public places and begged him, saying, "Just let us touch the tassel of your prayer shawl!" And all who touched him were instantly healed!*

Jesus had sent out the disciples to preach the good news. To heal the sick. To raise the dead. To cast out demons. This part of the story picks up where the disciples had returned. They told Jesus all the things they had done. All the people they had helped. All the teachings about Jesus they had done. Jesus wanted to take a break and have some quiet time for Him and the disciples. They left on a boat, but the people realized where they were going and chased after them. Surrounding towns joined in. By the time they arrived at the secluded place, a massive crowd was waiting.

Can you imagine that? Chasing after Jesus. Trying to get where he was going. Wanting to be close to Him so much that you ran after Him and went to a secluded spot in order to be there with Him. Just to be that close to Jesus would be awe inspiring. I can imagine with every shout of Yeshua, the Pharisees and other Jewish leaders became more and more jealous of the attention he was getting. As it increased, I imagine that the plots to get him also increased. The people, however, wanted Him. They wanted to be close to Him. To hear the words of the Master. To see Him help His people. The love that was poured out on Him.

Jesus, with all His compassion, taught them many wonderful things. What were those wonderful things? Man, I would love to see and hear what He said to them. The power of His words. The love and compassion coming out of Him. The words piercing the hearts of men. No wonder they crowded Him. Tried to stay around Him.

Wanted to be close to Him. Their spirits were crying out for the living Son of God that was right in front of them.

There was an issue though. Food. The people were around Him so long and He was ministering so long that they did not eat. They were so consumed with chasing Jesus that they did not bring food with them. Oh, to be that consumed with Jesus! The disciples started asking Jesus to send away the people to go into the towns and buy some food. Jesus replied, "You give them something to eat." I can imagine that Jesus had a smile on His face when he said this. He was about to change their perception again. They looked in the natural for food rather than looking to the one who could provide.

They had five loaves of bread and two fishes. That is it. The Bible says there were over five thousand men plus women and children. Let's back up in the story a minute. Jesus and the Disciples got on a boat and tried to go to a secluded place. The townspeople from several towns pursued Jesus in that secluded place. The numbers were five thousand men plus women and children. Logic would suggest that the total number was way over ten thousand counting their wives and children. So well over ten thousand people pursued Jesus at that moment! These days we cannot seem to get people fully engaged at church or even go to church. Yet, these ten thousand plus people chased Jesus and His disciples for who knows how long. What would it look like if every Christian had this much passion for Jesus? What would it look like if even half of Christians had that much passion for Jesus?

Back to the story. They had five loaves of bread and two fish. Over ten thousand people and they had five loaves of bread and two fish. If my math is correct, that is not going to work. There are a ton of people not going to eat if my calculations are correct. Seriously, what can you do there? It is not like you have enough food for eight people and have 10 guests, so you spread it around enough for everyone. They had a serious lack here. However, Jesus was there.

Would He tell them to go into town and ask for food? There is no way they could afford to buy that much food. With that many people, they could not put undue hardship on the towns trying to get enough food for that many people. Jesus had a better idea. He prayed over the food, broke the bread, and distributed the food out to the disciples to give to the groups of people. The food multiplied right in front of them. The food multiplied right in front of them. **The food multiplied right in front of them.**

Can you wrap your head around that? What were the disciples thinking when they saw the food multiply right in front of them? What was the crowd thinking when they saw this? The food just kept coming. The Bible says everyone had plenty to eat and was fully satisfied. In the end, each of the twelve disciples had a basket of leftovers. They went from not having enough for no more than ten to fifteen people and having to feed over ten thousand to have twelve baskets of leftovers after feeding every single person there! What an amazing story! A story of pursuing Jesus, and Jesus supplying our needs, His compassion, and His love for His people. These people did not care or even think about food when they started chasing Jesus. All they thought about was their pursuit of Him.

Afterwards, Jesus sent his disciples out on a boat, and He went up on the mountain to pray. Night fell and a storm had come. The waves were horrendous. This lasted until almost morning. Jesus came to them, walking on the water. When they saw Him, they thought it was a ghost and screamed out in terror. Totally gripped by fear. Jesus told them not to be gripped by fear for he was there, the Great I am.

Matthew's account of this story included Peter's response to Jesus. He said if it was really you, let me come out to you. Peter's faith in Jesus, although short-lived, made it possible for him to walk on water. Peter started panicking and lost his faith in an instant and started drowning. In walking on water and commanding the water to be still, Jesus demonstrated Himself to be in command of the natural world. He showed something that only God could do. What a couple of miracles! The Bible says when Jesus climbed in the boat, the waters became still. They were completely and utterly overwhelmed with astonishment. Overwhelmed with astonishment. That is a level of awe and wonder beyond description.

What were they thinking as they watched Jesus calming the storm? What was Peter thinking when he stepped out onto the water? The story is basically a miracle inside another miracle. Jesus was walking on water then calming the storms all in one sequence. Amazing! In the midst of an awful storm. Waves crashing on the boat. The boat was thrown about. They were absolutely in danger if not for Jesus. Then you look at Peter. Such strong faith if only short-lived. He started looking at his surroundings and allowed fear in. He saw the storm, the waves, and the danger. He took his eyes off Jesus and lost his way. He lost his strong faith.

What can we learn from this? First of all, Jesus is Lord of all. He is the master of the wind, the waves, and all the natural elements on Earth. He is in control so why worry. Second, Peter showed us what happens when we take our eyes off Jesus. When we take our eyes off Jesus, fear comes in. Our surroundings do not dictate our relationship with Jesus. Our surroundings do not take away from the fact that Jesus is in control. What is happening in our lives should NEVER dictate our level of trust, faith, or worship of Jesus. The bottom line, never, ever take your eyes off Jesus!!

The awe and wonder moment for me here was the story inside the story. From town to town people brought out their sick. Their afflicted. Their demonized. Jesus healed them all. Even the ones too sick to be on a mat, Jesus healed them. Absolutely astounding! All those people hurting, sick, in pain, in need of a healer and here came Jesus. His compassion and His love for them was so immense that he healed every last one of them. What would it be like to see the streets lined with sick people and Jesus walking through them healing them one by one? You see people down the street one by one standing up, completely healed. Extraordinary! The unimaginable scene coming to life seeing lines of people healed instantly.

## 10

## The Canaanite woman and feeding thousands

Speaking of incredible faith, there was the story of the Canaanite woman. She showed Jesus a level of faith he had not seen.

*Matthew 15- TPT* *21 Then Jesus left and went north into the non-Jewish region of Lebanon. 22 He encountered there a Canaanite woman who shouted out to him, "Lord, Son of David, show mercy to me! My daughter is horribly afflicted by a demon that torments her." 23 But Jesus never answered her. So his disciples said to him, "Why do you ignore this woman who is crying out to us?"*

*24 Jesus said, "I've only been sent to the lost sheep of Israel." 25 But she came and bowed down before him and said, "Lord, help me!"*

*26 Jesus responded, "It's not right for a man to take bread from his children and throw it out to the dogs."*

*27 "You're right, Lord," she replied. "But even puppies get to eat the crumbs that fall from the prince's table."*

*28 Then Jesus answered her, "Dear woman, your faith is strong! What you desire will be done for you." And at that very moment, her daughter was instantly set free from demonic torment.*

²⁹ After leaving Lebanon, Jesus went to Lake Galilee and climbed a hill nearby and sat down. ³⁰ Then huge crowds of people streamed up the hill, bringing with them the lame, blind, deformed, mute, and many others in need of healing. They laid them at Jesus' feet and he healed them all.

³¹ And the crowds marveled with amazement, astounded over the things they were witnessing with their own eyes! The lame were walking, the mute were speaking, the crippled were made well, and the blind could see. For three days everyone celebrated the miracles as they exalted and praised the God of Israel!

³² Jesus called his disciples to himself and said, "I care deeply about all these people, for they've already been with me for three days without food. I don't want to send them away fasting or else they may be overcome by weakness on their journey home."

³³ The disciples said to him, "Where in the world are we going to find enough food in this desolate place to feed this crowd?"

³⁴ "How many barley loaves do you have?" Jesus asked.

"Seven," they replied, "and a few small fish."

³⁵ So he gave the order, "Have the people sit down on the grass." ³⁶ Then he took the seven loaves and the fish and gave thanks to God. He broke the bread and gave it to his disciples, who then distributed the food to the crowds. ³⁷ When everyone was full and satisfied, they

*gathered up the leftovers. And from what was once seven loaves and a few fish, they filled seven baskets!* [38] *There were four thousand men who ate the food Jesus multiplied, and even more including the women and children!*

The Canaanite woman was desperate. She was coming to Jesus as a Mother. She was crying out for her child. Her child was tormented by a demon. What does that do to a mother seeing her child like this? How desperate would you be seeing your child like this? She begged for mercy. She was asking for compassion. As a parent, I can't imagine what she was going through. As a parent, she poured out her anguish on Jesus asking Him to heal her daughter. For some reason, Jesus did not answer her. Why? I am sure there is a lot of speculation as to why. Many experts with their theories. Did he ignore her waiting for her show of faith? Did he ignore her because he didn't hear her in the crowds? Did he ignore her because he really was focused on the Jews? This will be a question for Jesus when we sit with Him, dine with Him, and walk with Him.

Nevertheless, He did ignore her. Even the Disciples asked why He was ignoring the woman. He did test people, however, to prove their intentions with challenges or questions. He had never ignored someone before that we know of. He always showed an amazing amount of love and compassion. His Disciples questioned Him. The Canaanite woman bowed before Jesus. She pleaded with Him again, "Lord, help me!" Twice she pleaded with Him. Twice.

Jesus's response was definitely not something that anyone expected. "It's not right for a man to take bread from his children and throw it out to the dogs." Was she called a dog? Was Jesus insulting her? I don't think so. It was a metaphor of Jesus prioritizing his ministry to the Jews.

He was not saying she was a dog, in my opinion. He used a dog as a metaphor because Jews often refer to Gentiles as dogs. I believe this was a way, again, to gauge their intentions. The Canaanite woman could have taken offense to the dog comment. She could have said, forget you. She could have got up and left. She was not going to be denied. Even if she was offended, her desire for her daughter to be healed was greater than being offended. This is a valuable lesson for us all. Keep our eyes on the ultimate goal, our ultimate desire, and not let the things of this world, the issues of this world, the actions of others, or anything else deter you from that goal.

Her response was incredible. "You're right, Lord," she replied. "But even puppies get to eat the crumbs that fall from the prince's table." What an awesome statement! She was tugging on Jesus's compassion strings. The heartfelt cry of a mother begging for mercy from Jesus. The level of faith this woman had was amazing! Jesus acknowledged her strong faith with His response. "Dear woman, your faith is strong! What you desire will be done for you." In an instant, he spoke words of power, compassion, love, and healing. The Canaanite woman's faith, desire, and cry moved Jesus's heart to heal her daughter.

I wonder, what moves Jesus's heart? What does He want? What is His desire? What would it take to make Him sit forward on His throne? What can we do to move His heart? What can we do to please Him? What pleases His heart? Oh, how I long to move His heart. How I long to please Him! The Bible says the daughter was instantly healed. There is that word again, instant. Instant. Immediate healing. This is the case throughout Jesus's ministry. Instant healing. Amazing stories after amazing stories. The awe of Jesus! Awe of His power. Awe of His authority. Awe of His compassion. Awe of His love for us!

After this amazing story, Jesus left there and went to Lake Galilee. Crowds of people followed Him. Thousands wanted to be close to Him. They wanted to see more of Him. They wanted to hear more from Him. They were not concerned with anything else. They were consumed by Him. They wanted more of Him. They knew he was more than a man. They knew he was more than a Jew. They knew they had to be with Him. Be close to Him. Taught by Him. Then the Bible says *then huge crowds of people streamed up the hill, bringing with them the lame, blind, deformed, mute, and many others in need of healing. They laid them at Jesus' feet and he healed them all.*

People in need of healing, huge crowds of them, laying at Jesus's feet. Jesus healed them all. No matter the disease, sickness, issue, how bad or how long. They marveled with amazement. Astounded by what they were seeing. They were in awe of what they were witnessing. The miracles. The healings. The deliverances. The lame were walking. Walking! What would it be like to go from not being able to walk to fully healed and walking? I can imagine they were running. Jumping. Leaping for joy! The blind could see! What would it be like to be blind then one day , one moment, in an instant, they could see and the first thing they saw was the face of Jesus! The sweet face of the Messiah. The love and compassion in His eyes. The power of God flowing through Him. Unbelievable! The mute in an instant speaking! Going from not being able to speak to being able to open their mouth and praise the Lord, right to Jesus's face! Can you imagine it? How loud would a person's praise be if they hadn't been able to talk for a long time or even forever then in an instant talk, scream, shout, call on the name of Jesus!

The Bible says *For three days everyone celebrated the miracles as they exalted and praised the God of Israel!* For 3 days people were joyous. They were shouting, praising God. Their Messiah had come. People were healed. People were freed. A three-day celebration of Jesus. What did that look like? They didn't worry about food. They didn't worry about jobs, money, or other normal life stuff. It was a celebration beyond any celebration has ever been. What would it be like to spend three straight days worshiping Jesus with Jesus in person? With thousands upon thousands of people how loud was that party? What would it be like to be a part of that celebration? For those three days, all was perfect. No worries about the Romans. Not worrying about their next meal, their income, sickness, disabilities, absolutely nothing! Three days of Heaven on Earth similarities.

Jesus knew that the people had not eaten in 3 days. He was concerned that some of them would not make it, not eating for three days then traveling home. They were in a desolate place. No major towns close to get food, especially for that many people. The Bible says there were over four thousand men plus women and children. Logically that would put it over ten thousand people. That would be a ton of food needed to feed that many people. In the middle of nowhere, nearly no food, no ability to get food, and four thousand men plus women and children have not eaten for three days. Celebration over. They had 7 barley loaves and a few small fish. Enough food for say, 5 people, maybe 10 people? They need enough food for ten thousand. They are about to see yet another miracle.

Jesus prayed over the food, broke the bread and gave out to the Disciples to feed the crowd. These people had not eaten in at least 3 days. They had to be starving. A small meal wasn't going to cut it. Just a normal amount of food wouldn't cut it. I can imagine they all were ready to eat a significant amount of food. The Bible says they all ate until they were full and satisfied. After that, the leftovers filled seven baskets. Jesus's miracle fed four thousand men plus women and children then gave them seven baskets of leftovers. His compassion and love for His people went beyond just healings and deliverances. He wanted to take care of them naturally as well. His thoughts were continually on the people's overall well-being. It is the same today. He is always looking out for our well-being.

My awe and wonder moment here was the mother crying out for her child. No insult, mocking, denial, or ignoring of her words was going to stop her. It was an inner cry of her heart, a mother's heart that spoke to Jesus. His compassion for her and her child was immeasurable. His love for her and her child was vast. The awe of Jesus's level of compassion and love for us cannot even be described. Astounding! Our feeble minds cannot wrap around how much he loves us. How much he adores us. How much he delights in us.

## 11

## His mercy & Peter's revelation of Jesus

*Mark 10-TPT. 46 When Jesus and his disciples had passed through Jericho, a large crowd joined them. Upon leaving the village, they met a blind beggar sitting on the side of the road named Timai, the son of Timai. 47 When he heard that Jesus from Nazareth was passing by, he began to shout "Jesus, son of David, have mercy on me now in my affliction. Heal me!"*

*48 Those in the crowd were indignant and scolded him for making so much of a disturbance, but he kept shouting with all his might, "Son of David, have mercy on me now and heal me!"*

*49 Jesus stopped and said, "Call him here." So they went to the blind man and said, "Have courage! Get up! Jesus is calling for you!" 50 So he threw off his beggars' cloak, jumped up, and made his way to Jesus.*

*51 Jesus said to him, "What do you want me to do for you?"*

*The man replied, "My Master, please, let me see again!"*

*52 Jesus responded, "Your faith heals you. Go in peace, with your sight restored." All at once, the man's eyes opened and he could see again, and he began at once to follow Jesus, walking down the road with him.*

Jesus, once again, had large crowds around Him. He had droves of people trying to get close to Him. Desperately trying to get their healing, their deliverance, or just want to be close to the Messiah. Their hearts dance as they get close to Him. The one thing they have longed for is there. Everything they hoped for is standing in front of them and He is delivering on every prophecy from the Old Testament. He brought them hope. He brought them love. He brought them compassion. He brought them mercy. He brought them everything the religious leaders did not.

Jesus came across a blind beggar. As soon as he heard Jesus was passing by, he started shouting out. He cried out for mercy as he acknowledged who Jesus was, the Son of David. He asked Jesus to heal him. He did not say, if you can heal me. He didn't ask can you heal me. He was positive Jesus could heal him. He did not care what it looked like. He was shouting trying to get Jesus's attention. He was shouting to get his voice above the crowds of people around Jesus. He was desperate. He wanted his healing and was going to do everything he could to get it.

The blind beggar was yelling. He was not doing some soft little prayer. He was not being passive. It was a desperate cry for help. A desperate cry for mercy. A desperate cry for healing. A cry out from a desperate man. He asked for Jesus's mercy. I wonder how many times over the time that he was a blind beggar did he ask the Jewish leaders for help. For mercy. I imagine he asked. This was his appointed time though, a time with Jesus. His life was about to change, forever.

The people in the crowd tried to shut him up. I'm sure they probably heard him before, asking for help. Asking for mercy. Instead of help, he got scolded for making a disturbance. Disturbance? Crowds of people were following Jesus, pressed up against Him. I imagine the crowds were not silent so there was noise. Yet they complain about this man making a disturbance. Really? I personally think they thought the blind beggar was less of a person since he was blind, on the street, begging. They sure treated him as less of a person. Jesus, however, did not.

Again, he yelled out for mercy. He yelled out for healing. This time Jesus says to bring the blind beggar to him. I can imagine how Jesus felt hearing the crowd telling the man to be quiet. How Jesus felt seeing his people treat the blind beggar as less of a person. His compassion and His love paved the way for this man. He asked him what he could do for him. The blind beggar said he wanted to see again. Jesus healed him. Instantly. In an instant, the man went from blind to seeing the face of Jesus! In an instant, he went from blind beggar to follower of Jesus.

Then there was the story of Peter's revelation of Jesus. What powerful words...

*Matt 16- TPT* [13] *When Jesus came to Caesarea Philippi, he asked his disciples this question: "What are the people saying about me, the Son of Man? Who do they believe I am?"*

[14] *They answered, "Some are convinced you are John the Baptizer, others say you are Elijah reincarnated, or Jeremiah, or one of the prophets."*

[15] *"But you—who do you say that I am?" Jesus asked.*

[16] *Simon Peter spoke up and said, "You are the Anointed One, the Son of the living God!"*

[17] *Jesus replied, "You are favored and privileged Simeon, son of Jonah! For you didn't discover this on your own, but my Father in heaven has supernaturally revealed it to you.* [18] *I give you the name Peter, a stone. And this rock will be the bedrock foundation on which I will build my church—my legislative assembly, and the power of death will not be able to overpower it!* [19] *I will give you the keys of heaven's kingdom realm to forbid on earth that which is forbidden in heaven, and to release on earth that which is released in heaven."* [20] *He then gave his disciples strict orders not to tell anyone that he was the Messiah.*

This was a turning point in Jesus's ministry. Up to this point, he avoided using words such as Messiah or Christ. Jesus knew how it would cause issues with religious leaders. He first asked what others said about who he was. They gave him all sorts of answers.

John the Baptist. Elijah. Jeremiah. One of the prophets. No, no, no, and no. Their thought process was of men. Then Jesus asked his disciples, who do you say that I am? His inner circle. The ones closest to Him. The ones that have been with Him since the beginning. The ones that saw countless miracles of healings, deliverances, and more.

Then Peter said one of the most powerful statements in the Bible. ""You are the Anointed One, the Son of the living God!" I wonder if there was thunder or any loud rumblings when he said that? I wonder if demons shook and trembled at that sentence? I wonder if the Earth quaked at this statement? I wonder if the disciples fell down at that statement and worshiped Him? The revelation of Jesus as the Messiah with those words spoken out is awesome. Those words took Jesus from being seen as a Jew, a prophet, John the Baptist or any other man to the Messiah. The Holy One. The Anointed One.

This transition along with the Transfiguration truly put Jesus on the path to Jerusalem where his death, burial, and resurrection awaits Him. The Transfiguration is an amazing story and description of Jesus.

*Matt 17-TPT*   *17 Six days later Jesus took Peter and the two brothers, Jacob and John, and hiked up a high mountain to be alone. 2 Then Jesus' appearance was dramatically altered. A radiant light as bright as the sun poured from his face. And his clothing became luminescent—dazzling like lightning. He was transfigured before their very eyes.* ³ *Then suddenly, Moses and Elijah appeared, and they spoke with Jesus.*

⁴ *Peter blurted out, "Lord, it's so wonderful that we are all here together! If you want, I'll construct three shrines, one for you, one for Moses, and one for Elijah."*

⁵ *But while Peter was still speaking, a bright radiant cloud spread over them, enveloping them all. And God's voice suddenly spoke from the cloud, saying, "This is my dearly loved Son, the constant focus of my delight. Listen to him!"*

⁶ *The three disciples were dazed and terrified by this phenomenon, and they fell facedown to the ground.* ⁷ *But Jesus walked over and touched them, saying, "Get up and stop being afraid."* ⁸ *When they finally opened their eyes and looked around, they saw no one else there but Jesus.*

⁹ *As they all hiked down the mountain together, Jesus ordered them, "Don't tell anyone of the divine appearance you just witnessed. Wait until the Son of Man is raised from the dead."*

¹⁰ *His disciples asked him, "Why do all the religious scholars insist that Elijah must first appear before the Anointed One comes?"*

¹¹ *He answered them, "They're right. Elijah must come first and restore all things.* ¹² *But Elijah has already appeared. And yet they*

*didn't recognize him, so they did to him whatever they pleased. And the Son of Man is destined to suffer the same abuse as what they did to him."*

*¹³ Then the disciples realized that Jesus was referring to John the Baptizer all along.*

What an amazing story! To see Jesus' transfiguration would be indescribable. He took only 3 of his closest disciples high up on the mountain. He showed them a glimpse of his Heavenly form. The radiant light was as bright as the sun pouring from His face. His clothes were dazzling like lightning. What did that look like? How incredible would it be to witness this? The glory and the splendor of Jesus all around Him. Did the ground shake? Did thunder roll? Did they hear the sounds of Heaven with this? Then, just as you think it couldn't get any more amazing, Moses and Elijah appeared. What? Really? Moses and Elijah? Not only do they get to see Jesus in his glory, all his splendor, then see Moses and Elijah. Unbelievable.

Peter blurted out, asking Jesus if it pleases him, they will build shrines to each of them. As Peter spoke a cloud surrounded them all. A bright radiant cloud. the cloud enveloped them all. God spoke and said this was His son, and he is very pleased with Him. Listen to Him. So let's summarize the story up to this point from the disciples' viewpoint. First, they see Jesus, transfigured in all His glory, then they get to see Moses and Elijah. If all of that is not enough, they hear the audible voice of God in the bright cloud surrounding them. What an amazing series of events! What did they see? How did God's voice sound? What did it look like seeing the bright clouds with God's voice coming out of it?

After that, they came down off the mountain where all of that happened. Yet another opportunity for Jesus to show his compassion, love, and healing power.

*Matt 17- TPT* *14* *They came to where a large crowd had gathered to wait for Jesus. A man came and knelt before him* *15* *and said, "Lord, please show your tender mercy toward my son. He has a demon who afflicts him. He has epilepsy, and he suffers horribly from seizures. He often falls into the cooking fire or into the river.* *16* *I brought him to your followers, but they weren't able to heal him."*

*17* *Jesus replied, "Where is your faith? Can't you see how wayward and wrong this generation is? How much longer do I stay with you and put up with your doubts? Bring your son to me."*

*18* *Then Jesus rebuked the demon and it came out of him and the boy was instantly healed!*

*19* *Later the disciples came to him privately and asked, "Why couldn't we cast out the demon?"*

*[20] He told them, "It was because of your lack of faith. I promise you, if you have faith inside of you no bigger than the size of a small mustard seed, you can say to this mountain, 'Move away from here and go over there,' and you will see it move! There is nothing you couldn't do! [21] But this kind is cast out only through prayer and fasting."*

Another example of parental desperation. His son had epilepsy. He was having seizures. He was falling into fires or water. He was suffering. Something needed to be done. He brought them to the disciples previously, but they could not heal him. However, he did not give up. He was determined to get his son help. He asked for mercy from Jesus. Kneeling before Jesus pleading for Him to heal his son. Jesus seems to get irritated with the situation and the fact that the disciples could not heal him.

He talked about their lack of faith. He had them bring the boy to him. Jesus healed him, again, instantly. Privately, the disciples asked about why they could not heal him. Jesus explained about their lack of faith, what could happen with strong faith, and how the boy was healed. Instantly. It was almost a father-like teaching for the disciples. His compassion and love for the boy was amazing.

My awe and wonder moment has to be the Transfiguration. What did that look like? To see the Glory of God around Him. What an honor to be able to see something so special. To see Jesus in all His glory. To see Moses and Elijah. Stunning. What did they talk about? How bright was the light surrounding Him? Did they hear the sounds of Heaven while this was going on? Did they hear anything? Did they see anything else? So many thoughts here. Just overwhelming to think about what they were seeing.

## 12

## The Triumphal Entry & cleansing the temple

Then comes the Triumphant entry. The Holy One. The Messiah enters Jerusalem. He is worshiped like the King he is. Jesus sent them to get a colt that was tied up in Jerusalem.

*Luke 19- TPT* *[35-36] After they brought the colt to Jesus, they placed their prayer shawls on its back, and Jesus rode it as he descended the Mount of Olives toward Jerusalem. As he rode toward the city, people spontaneously threw their prayer shawls like a carpet on the path in front of him.*

*[37] As soon as he got to the bottom of the Mount of Olives, the crowd of his followers shouted with a loud outburst of ecstatic joy over all the mighty wonders of power they had witnessed. [38] They shouted over and over, "Highest praises to God for the one who comes as King in the name of the Lord! Heaven's peace and glory from the highest realm now comes to us!"*

*[39] Some Jewish religious leaders who stood off from the procession said to Jesus, "Teacher, order your followers at once to stop saying these things!"*

*[40] Jesus responded, "Listen to me. If my followers were silenced, the very stones would break forth with praises!"*

*⁴¹ When Jesus caught sight of the city, he burst into tears with uncontrollable weeping over Jerusalem, ⁴² saying, "If only you could recognize that this day peace is within your reach! But you cannot see it. ⁴³ For the day is soon coming when your enemies will surround you, hem you in on every side, and lay siege to you. ⁴⁴ They will crush you to pieces, and your children too! And they will leave your city totally destroyed. Since you would not recognize God's day of visitation, you will see your day of devastation!"*

*⁴⁵ Jesus entered the temple area and forcibly threw out all the merchants from their stalls. ⁴⁶ He rebuked them, saying, "The Scriptures declare, 'My Father's house is to be filled with prayer— a house of prayer, not a cave of bandits!' "*

*⁴⁷ From then on Jesus continued teaching in the temple area, but the high priests, the experts of the law, and the prominent men of the city kept trying to find a strategy to accuse Jesus, for they wanted him dead. ⁴⁸ They could find no reason to accuse him, for he was a hero to the people and the crowds were awestruck by every word he spoke.*

Jesus' entry into Jerusalem was now what we know as Palm Sunday. This is one week away from Jesus' crucifixion. The Jews laid their cloaks down. They laid prayer shawls down. They laid palm branches down. Some waved them to Jesus. In Mark and in Luke, the Bible says they shouted things like:

"Bring in the Victory"

"We welcome the one coming with blessings sent from the Lord Yahweh!"

"Blessings rest on this kingdom he ushers in—the kingdom of our father David! "

"Bring us the victory in the highest realms *of heaven*!"

"Highest praises to God for the one who comes as King in the name of the Lord!"

"Heaven's peace and glory from the highest realm *now comes to us*!"

It was a celebration! The Messiah was there, in Jerusalem! The King of Glory has arrived. Oh, to be able to see that majestic sight would be amazing! The crowds of people praising Jesus. Hailing the King of Kings. Did they bow down and worship Him?

Did they cry, knowing that the Messiah they had waited for and heard prophecies about was there? Life would never be the same. Everything was changing. The greatest event throughout all history was happening right in front of them. He entered Jerusalem with indescribable love for us. He rode in on a colt surrounded by an endless number of people with their love pouring out on Him.

It is important to note that Jesus had foreknowledge of the coming events and knew the colt would be there AND the owner would allow Jesus to borrow it. The lesson here is in fact Jesus did know what was going to happen. He knew that he was going to go to the cross and he did so willingly. He was not a victim of the events unfolding but he knew his Father's plan for Him and he gave it all to accomplish it. His love for us was greater than what he was about to go through. Jesus was deliberately fulfilling prophecy from Zechariah chapter 9. Jesus was proclaiming Himself as the promised King of Israel. The Messiah.

The strange thing for the Jews was when He came into Jerusalem. It was strange to them because he wasn't the King they expected. They expected the Son of God to establish God's kingdom on Earth and rid them of the Romans. Jesus was the opposite of what they thought He was going to be. He never came against the Romans. In fact, he never gave them much mind. Never spoke against them, yelled at them, or anything else for that matter. he didn't come to fight the Romans. He came to deliver the world from sin. He came to restore God's honor. He came as an expression of His love for us.

Some of the Jewish leaders told Jesus to tell the people to stop saying the things they were saying. They were offended by the people worshiping Him, praising Him, calling him King, Yahweh, and many more names. How could anyone tell Jesus to do this? How ridiculous is this request? Did they really think they would stop? The King of Kings, the Lord of Lords, the Messiah is right in front of them riding a colt into Jerusalem and they think people are going to stop worshiping Him? The Anointed One who raised the little girl, a little boy, Lazarus, and who knows who else from the dead. The one that delivered countless people from demons. The one that healed lepers, made the blind see, made the deaf hear, the lame to walk and they want people to stop praising Jesus?

How could they do this? How could anyone stop worshiping Him? How could they treat Jesus this way? How could anyone ever treat Jesus the way they did? With all His love, all His compassion, they want to harm Him? Jesus has the perfect response though. "Listen to me. If my followers were silenced, the very stones would break forth with praises!" This drop the mic moment is brought to you by Jesus. Even the rocks cry out for the living God!

Jesus entered the temple. It is important to note this is not the same day as the triumphal entry. Jesus looked around. He saw the selling inside the temple. The trade that was going on in the Holy

Temple. People would come purchasing animals for sacrifice. They would exchange currencies. They would only allow one coin in the temple. This was done with the approval of the priests. Some scholars speculated that they even had their hand in the pot, taking their cut. Also, some scholars believe that the ones that would sell sacrifice animals were scam artists as well. They speculate that they would sell the animal for sacrifice then when the person takes the animal to be sacrificed, they would not do it. They would bring it back out to the tables to re-sell them.

Jesus saw what was going on in the temple. It was supposed to be a holy place. A place for prayer. A place to be with God. These people turned it into a den of thieves. These innocent people come to the holy temple only to be taken advantage of. Sound familiar? The big difference is on that particular day, Jesus was there. He showed them a holy anger because of what they did in God's house. He flipped over the tables. He scolded them for their deeds. One by one he exited them out of the temple. The love of money overtook them. They were taking advantage of people in the house of God. Two thousand years later, sadly this is still going on in many churches. The priests conspired ways to execute Jesus, but they had to be careful as Jesus was a hero to the people. The crowds were awestruck by Jesus. They were captivated by his teachings.

The awe and wonder moment in this chapter is definitely the triumphal entry. What an entrance! Jesus, the Messiah. The

Anointed One. The Holy King. The Great healer. All the people, worshiping Jesus. Hail to the King! They laid down prayer shawls. They celebrated their King coming into Jerusalem. I could only imagine. Seeing Jesus riding the colt. All His majesty, all His glory. Thousands worshiping Him. Talk about an awesome moment!

## 13

## The alabaster jar, forgiveness, & true worship

One of my favorite stories in the New Testament is the story of the woman with the alabaster jar.

*Luke 7-TPT* [36] *Afterward Simeon, a Jewish religious leader, asked Jesus to his home for dinner. Jesus accepted the invitation. When he went to Simeon's home, he took his place at the table.*

[37] *In the neighborhood there was an immoral woman of the streets, known to all to be a prostitute. When she heard that Jesus was at Simeon's house, she took an exquisite flask made from alabaster, filled it with the most expensive perfume, went right into the home of the Jewish religious leader, and in front of all the guests, she knelt at the feet of Jesus.* [38] *Broken and weeping, she covered his feet with the tears that fell from her face. She kept crying and drying his feet with her long hair. Over and over she kissed Jesus' feet. Then, as an act of worship, she opened her flask and anointed his feet with her costly perfume.*

[39] *When Simeon saw what was happening, he thought, "This man can't be a true prophet. If he were really a prophet, he would know what kind of sinful woman is touching him."*

[40] *Jesus said, "Simeon, I have a word for you."*

*"Go ahead, Teacher. I want to hear it," he answered.*

*⁴¹ "It's a story about two men who were deeply in debt. One owed the bank one hundred thousand dollars, and the other only owed ten thousand dollars. ⁴² When it was obvious that neither of them would be able to repay their debts, the kind banker graciously wrote off the debts and forgave them all that they owed. Tell me, Simeon, which of the two debtors would be more thankful? Which one would love the banker most?"*

*⁴³ Simeon answered, "I suppose it would be the one with the greater debt forgiven."*

*"You're right," Jesus agreed. ⁴⁴ Then he spoke to Simeon about the woman still weeping at his feet.*

*"Do you see this woman kneeling here? She is doing for me what you didn't bother to do. When I entered your home as your guest, you didn't think about offering me water to wash the dust off my feet. Yet she came into your home and washed my feet with her many tears and then dried my feet with her hair. ⁴⁵ You didn't even welcome me into your home with the customary kiss of greeting, but from the moment I came in she has not stopped kissing my feet. ⁴⁶ You didn't take the time to anoint my head with fragrant oil, but she anointed my head and feet with the finest perfume. ⁴⁷ She has been forgiven of all her many sins. This is why she has shown me such*

*extravagant love. But those who assume they have very little to be forgiven will love me very little."*

<sup>48</sup> *Then Jesus said to the woman at his feet, "All your sins are forgiven."*

<sup>49</sup> *All the dinner guests said among themselves, "Who is the one who can even forgive sins?"*

<sup>50</sup> *Then Jesus said to the woman, "Your faith in me has given you life. Now you may leave and walk in the ways of peace."*

What an amazing story! Jesus accepted an invitation from Simeon to come to his house for dinner. When Jesus arrived, no one offered him water to wash his feet, which was customary at that time. He was not greeted with the customary kiss. They did nothing to welcome him into their home. These were customary actions to welcome a guest. A guest. They were welcoming Jesus into their home.

Some scholars believe that it was an effort to mistreat Him as an attempt to dishonor Him in hopes that people would lose interest in following Him. Very possible in my opinion. The Jewish leaders have been conspiring ways to kill him so it is very possible this was all a set up. What started out as an opportunity to treat Jesus poorly, turned into a beautiful scene of worship, love, and forgiveness. All the guests there, inside and outside the home. All of them witnessed how Jesus was being treated.

One person that witnessed how Jesus was being treated was the former prostitute. She found out Jesus was at Simeon's house and went and got an alabaster jar and filled it with very expensive perfume. She arrived at Simeon's house. I can imagine her shock, her disgust at the way Jesus was being treated. It is important to note as a known prostitute, she was probably not welcome in their home. They knew what she was. Jesus saw her for what he created her to be.

I can imagine her running into the room, plowing through the people. Pushing people out of the way. Those people that were disrespecting Jesus. She decided she wasn't going to let them treat Jesus this way. She fell at his feet, sobbing. Her tears washed Jesus's feet. Over and over kissing Jesus' feet. Then she did something even more offensive to the people in attendance. She took that bottle of expensive perfume and poured it out on Jesus' feet and head. In an amazing act of worship, she anointed Jesus.

Broken, she came to Jesus. She knew who he was. She knew He was the only one that could help her change her life. She was a sinner in need of Jesus. She knew that she wanted to show Him extravagant love. Most, if not everyone there, outside of Jesus thought this was foolish. They condemned her for it. Some said they could sell it and give the money to the poor. I can imagine all the whispering. The mocking. The shock that Jesus did not say anything about this woman, a known prostitute, is touching Him. This is still true today. You do something that many think is outrageous for the Lord and you get a lot of condemnation, sitting down, judgmental looks, whispering, gossiping, and more.

Jesus told the host, Simeon, a story. This was a story of forgiveness and one being forgiven of a larger debt than the other. All during the story, the woman was still weeping at his feet. What would that be like? At the feet of Jesus, weeping. The love pouring out of you. I can only imagine what that would be like. Words could not even describe. Jesus told them that she had been forgiven of her sins. They were many, which is why she was showing Jesus such extravagant love. He then went on to say the ones that think they have so little to be forgiven for will love him little. This is similar to today. Some Christians think their crap doesn't stink. They look at others with their judgmental looks, talking about their sins, their issues, their problems. Unfortunately, it turns people away from Jesus because they see them as hypocritical Christians.

This entire story was a picture of true worship. Giving what you have to Him. Giving what is most valuable to Him. Pouring out your love on Him. Not caring what you look like, what others think, only caring what Jesus thinks. Worshiping Him with everything inside you. When desperation takes over and you cannot go one more minute without worshiping Him. When the love inside you overwhelms you to the point you cannot help but to bust open your alabaster jar and pour it out on Jesus! When you cannot tell Him enough how much you love Him. How much you need Him.

The perfume cost an entire year's wage. An entire year! Her worship cost her a lot. She did not care. It was crazy. It was reckless. Breaking the very expensive jar. She could have just opened it but she broke it open. She gave everything to Him. She anointed Him in preparation for his burial. She took the opportunity to pour out her love on Him while He was still with them. Others could have joined her in worship. They could have honored the guest of honor with some type of respect. Instead, judgmental looks, sneering, mocking, and indignation. It did not matter to her though. Her only desire was to love on Him.

The awe and wonder here is this woman's privilege of pouring her love out on Jesus. She saw how Jesus was being treated. She didn't like it. She was going to worship Him as much as possible, right in front of them. She poured out her love on Him. He forgave her of her sins, and they were many. She was broken. She was weeping. Not just a few tears. Absolutely weeping. Tears falling down her face. Love pouring out of her. She knew her forgiveness was great. Her life would never be the same. She had one moment to show her love for Jesus, and she took it. It cost her a lot. A very expensive perfume is poured out on Him. It was her most valuable possession. It was ok with her. Jesus was worth it and more. What an awesome sight, Jesus being worshiped in front of people that wanted to demean Him. No matter what is going on around you, it should not stop your worship.

## 14

## Jesus washes feet, betrayal, & Peter's denial

We are getting closer to the final days of Jesus on Earth. He spent the time spending time with his most beloved followers.

*John 13- TPT 13 Jesus knew that the night before Passover would be his last night on earth before leaving this world to return to the Father's side. All throughout his time with his disciples, Jesus had demonstrated a deep and tender love for them. And now he longed to show them the full measure of his love. ² Before their evening meal had begun, the accuser had already deeply embedded betrayal into the heart of Judas Iscariot, the son of Simon.*

*³ Now Jesus was fully aware that the Father had placed all things under his control, for he had come from God and was about to go back to be with him. ⁴ So he got up from the meal and took off his outer robe, and took a towel and wrapped it around his waist. ⁵ Then he poured water into a basin and began to wash the disciples' dirty feet and dry them with his towel.*

*⁶ But when Jesus got to Simon Peter, he objected and said, "I can't let you wash my dirty feet—you're my Lord!"*

*⁷ Jesus replied, "You don't understand yet the meaning of what I'm doing, but soon it will be clear to you."*

*⁸ Peter looked at Jesus and said, "You'll never wash my dirty feet—never!"*

*"But Peter, if you don't allow me to wash your feet," Jesus responded, "then you will not be able to share life with me."*

*⁹ So Peter said, "Lord, in that case, don't just wash my feet, wash my hands and my head too!"*

*¹⁰ Jesus said to him, "You are already clean. You've been washed completely and you just need your feet to be cleansed—but that can't be said of all of you." For Jesus knew which one was about to betray him, ¹¹ and that's why he told them that not all of them were clean.*

*¹² After washing their feet, he put his robe on and returned to his place at the table. "Do you understand what I just did?" Jesus said. ¹³ "You've called me your teacher and lord, and you're right, for that's who I am. ¹⁴⁻¹⁵ So if I'm your teacher and lord and have just washed your dirty feet, then you should follow the example that I've set for you and wash one another's dirty feet. Now do for each other what I have just done for you. ¹⁶ I speak to you timeless truth: a servant is not superior to his master, and an apostle is never greater than the one who sent him. ¹⁷ So now put into practice what I have done for you, and you will experience a life of happiness enriched with untold blessings!"*

*¹⁸ "I don't refer to all of you when I tell you these things, for I know the ones I've chosen—to fulfill the Scripture that says, 'The one who shared supper with me treacherously betrays me.*[J] [19] *I am telling you this now, before it happens, so that when the prophecy comes to pass you will be convinced that I AM.* [20] *"Listen to this timeless truth: whoever receives the messenger I send receives me, and the one who receives me receives the Father who sent me."*

[21] *Then Jesus was moved deeply in his spirit. Looking at his disciples, he announced, "I tell you the truth—one of you is about to betray me."*

[22] *Eyeing each other, his disciples puzzled over which one of them could do such a thing.* [23] *The disciple that Jesus dearly loved was at the right of him at the table and was leaning his head on Jesus.* [24] *Peter gestured to this disciple to ask Jesus who it was he was referring to.* [25] *Then the dearly loved disciple leaned into Jesus' chest and whispered, "Master, who is it?"*

[26] *"The one I give this piece of bread to after I've dipped it in the bowl," Jesus replied. Then he dipped the piece of bread into the bowl and handed it to Judas Iscariot, the son of Simon.* [27] *And when Judas ate the piece of bread, Satan entered him. Then Jesus looked at Judas and said, "What you are planning to do, go do it now."* [28] *None of those around the table realized what was happening.* [29] *Some thought that Judas, their trusted treasurer, was being told to go buy what was needed for the Passover celebration, or perhaps to go give something to the poor.* [30] *So Judas left quickly and went out into the dark night to betray Jesus.*

$^{31}$ After Judas left the room, Jesus said, "The time has come for the glory of God to surround the Son of Man, and God will be greatly glorified through what happens to me. $^{32}$ And very soon God will unveil the glory of the Son of Man.

$^{33}$ "My dear friends, I only have a brief time left to be with you. And then you will search and long for me. But I tell you what I told the Jewish leaders: you'll not be able to come where I am.

$^{34}$ "So I give you now a new commandment: Love each other just as much as I have loved you. $^{35}$ For when you demonstrate the same love I have for you by loving one another, everyone will know that you're my true followers."

$^{36}$ Peter interjected, "But, Master, where are you going?"

Jesus replied, "Where I am going you won't be able to follow, but one day you will follow me there."

$^{37}$ Peter said, "What do you mean I'm not able to follow you now? I would sacrifice my life to die for you!"

$^{38}$ Jesus answered, "Would you really lay down your life for me, Peter? Here's the absolute truth: Before the rooster crows in the morning, you will say three times that you don't even know me!"

That first verse always gets me. It says "All throughout his time with his disciples, Jesus had demonstrated a deep and tender love for them. And now he longed to show them the full measure of his love." That statement is amazing and heart wrenching all at the same time. Jesus had a deep and tender love for them. Jesus has a deep and tender love for us. What an honor! It is an honor to have Jesus love us! It is even more marvelous that his love for us is that deep and tender. It brings me to tears when I think about this. I encourage you to pause for a minute and meditate on that for a minute. Jesus, the Son of the Living God, the Messiah, the Great I am, loves us deep and tender! Also, he showed his deep love to the fullest measure by what he did for us. Absolutely amazing!

The Bible then talks about how the accuser had already deeply embedded betrayal in Judas' heart. Jesus knew this already, yet he talked about his deep love for them. Unreal! Jesus, knowing what Judas was going to do showed his love for them, not contempt towards Judas. How many could say they would love on Judas knowing he was going to betray you? Most, if not all people would either be rude to him, question his motives, or at the very least ostracize him from the group. Jesus did not. He loved him as much as he did anyone else. That is a level of love that we should all strive to attain.

Then Jesus proceeded to wash the disciples' feet. Jesus washed their feet. Jesus did. How awkward would that be? The King, the Messiah, the Master, the Lord of all, washing their feet. He is the one that should be getting His feet washed! He deserves all our praise, the honor, the glory. He deserves all our worship.

Peter told Jesus he would never let Him wash his feet. I can understand that statement. I am not worthy of Jesus washing my feet. I am not worthy of Jesus doing anything for me. However, that is the level of love we don't understand fully. Matt 20:28 he revealed He came "not to be served but to serve, and to give his life as a ransom for many." Jesus' humility was on full display here. Jesus washes the feet of his followers. I am in awe of Jesus' love for his disciples. I am in more awe of His love for us! My feeble brain cannot completely wrap around the level of love He has for us. All of us. Every person. The horrible ones. The murderers. The adulterers. The rapists. The ones that mock Him, make fun of Him, deny His existence. He loves us all. He doesn't love some of the things we do, but his love never ceases!

Once Peter made that statement of Jesus never washing his feet, Jesus responded. He said, "But Peter, if you don't allow me to wash your feet, then you will not be able to share life with me." Peter had an amazing response! Peter said, "Lord, in that case, don't just wash my feet, wash my hands and my head too!" He was basically saying, I want it all!! I am completely sold out for you, and I want everything you have for me! Take every part of me! I give you everything! Pour it out on me!! That passionate statement is amazing! It showed Peter's level of passion for Jesus. Oh, for all of us to have that level of passion for Jesus! Jesus gave his all, all for love, and he deserves that same level of love, passion, and desire for Him!

Then came the hard part. Jesus made a statement that not everyone at the table was that passionate for Him. He said that one at the table was going to betray him, which fulfilled the Old Testament prophecy. Who would do such a thing? Who would betray Jesus? There are several theories as to why. One theory is that Judas did not betray Jesus rather Judas tried to build a bridge between the Jewish people and Jesus. The issue with this theory is Jesus would have to not know what Judas was doing. Another theory is Judas was evil from the beginning. There is certainly ample evidence in John to support this theory. However, there are some issues with this theory as well. If Judas was evil all along, why did Jesus choose him as a disciple? Why did he give him authority to heal? In the end, Judas went back to the Jewish leaders saying he betrayed innocent blood and gave the money back. If he was evil, he would not have remorse for his doings.

Another theory is Satan entered Judas. This is mentioned in Luke. None of the disciples knew he was the betrayer so signs point that Judas may have been a good disciple. After the betrayal, Satan left Judas, so his repentance was real and heartfelt. The final theory is that Judas tried to force Jesus' hand in taking over power in Israel and overthrowing the Romans. With everything that had happened, including his triumphal entry, he thought it was the perfect time to turn Jesus over in hopes that He would rise up and take power.

This will be a question that we will probably have to wait until we sit down with Jesus and ask Him. Each theory has its good and bad points. Either way, Jesus was betrayed by a person close to Him. I cannot comprehend as to why. All that they have seen. The miracles. The healings. The deliverances. They knew He was the Messiah. He was their King. He had done nothing but show love for His people. Compassion for His people, yet there was a betrayer in the midst.

Jesus knew what he was going to do. That is the amazing part. He knew what he was going to go through, but he did it anyway. His love was so great for us that he voluntarily went through it. To make it even more incredible, this story takes us to Peter. When Judas left to betray Jesus, Jesus turned his attention to Peter. Peter was listening to Jesus talk about how the glory of God will be revealed through what he was about to do and that they would not be able to go with Him. Peter asked Him where He was going. After Jesus told him he could not go with him, Peter said that he would sacrifice and die for Him. Jesus answered, "Would you really lay down your life for me, Peter? Here's the absolute truth: Before the rooster crows in the morning, you will say three times that you don't even know me!"

What a painful statement. "Would you really lay your life down for me?" That rhetorical question must have stung. Simply pierced his heart. The Lord that you spent all that time with, saw the miracles, saw the healings, love more than anything, questioning your loyalty and He is right. Then Jesus hammered it home by telling him before the rooster crows in the morning, you will deny me not once, not twice, but three times. That just hurts my heart. Denying Jesus. I understand why. It was fight or flight time and Peter chose flight. I understand I was not in his position but how could anyone do this? Those words must have cut like a knife. What did Peter Think about this? Was he offended? Did he deny what he was going to deny? At this point, it is words. Later we will review the rest of that story.

My awe and wonder moment here was Peter's denial of Jesus. Jesus knew he was going to deny Him. Yet, Jesus took everything he took. He knew how sinful man was and is throughout time, yet he completed his mission. He took it all. How could Peter deny Him? The things he saw. The miracles he saw. He saw the transfiguration. He saw Moses and Elijah. He saw the thousands fed. He knew who Jesus was. He was passionate about Jesus yet denied Him. Why? Self-preservation? Maybe. It is easy to say you would die for Him but when it is time to step up to the plate, it can prove more challenging. I am in awe of Jesus, what he took, even when they didn't deserve mercy. It is the same thing today. Jesus shows us forgiveness and mercy, even when we don't deserve it.

## 15

## Jesus in the Garden and His arrest

Jesus was in the garden of Gethsemane. The end story was about to start.

*Matt 26- TPT* *[36] Then Jesus led his disciples to an orchard called "The Oil Press." He told them, "Sit here while I go and pray nearby." [37] He took Peter, Jacob, and John with him. However, an intense feeling of great sorrow plunged his soul into agony. [38] And he said to them, "My heart is overwhelmed and crushed with grief. It feels as though I'm dying. Stay here and keep watch with me."*

*[39] Then he walked a short distance away, and overcome with grief, he threw himself facedown on the ground and prayed, "My Father, if there is any way you can deliver me from this suffering, please take it from me. Yet what I want is not important, for I only desire to fulfill your plan for me." Then an angel from heaven appeared to strengthen him.*

*[40] Later, he came back to his three disciples and found them all sound asleep. He awakened Peter and said to him, "Could you not stay awake with me for even one hour? [41] Keep alert and pray that you'll be spared from this time of testing. Your spirit is eager enough, but your humanity is weak."*

*42 Then he left them for a second time to pray in solitude. He said to God, "My Father, if there is not a way that you can deliver me from this suffering, then your will must be done."*

*43 He came back to the disciples and found them sound asleep, for they couldn't keep their eyes open. 44 So he left them and went away to pray the same prayer for the third time.*

*45 When he returned again to his disciples, he awoke them, saying, "Are you still sleeping? Don't you know the hour has come for the Son of Man to be handed over to the authority of sinful men? 46 Get up and let's go, for the betrayer has arrived."*

*47 At that moment Judas, his once-trusted disciple, appeared, along with a large crowd of men armed with swords and clubs. They had been sent to arrest Jesus by order of the ruling priests and Jewish religious leaders. 48 Now, Judas, the traitor, had arranged to give them a signal that would identify Jesus, for he had told them, "Jesus is the one whom I will kiss. So seize him!"*

*49 Judas quickly stepped up to Jesus and said, "Shalom, Rabbi," and he kissed him on both cheeks.*

*50 "My beloved friend," Jesus said, "is this why you've come?"*

*Then the armed men seized Jesus to arrest him. 51 But one of the disciples pulled out a dagger and swung it at the servant of the high priest, slashing off his ear. 52 Jesus said to him, "Put your dagger away. For all those who embrace violence will die by violence. ⁵³ Don't you realize that I could ask my heavenly Father for angels to come at any time to deliver me? And instantly he would answer me by sending more than twelve legions of angels to come and protect us. ⁵⁴ But that would thwart the prophetic plan of God. For it has been written that it would happen this way."*

*⁵⁵ Then Jesus turned to the mob and said, "Why would you arrest me with swords and clubs as though I were an outlaw? Day after day I sat in the temple courts with you, teaching the people, yet you didn't arrest me. ⁵⁶ But all of this fulfills the prophecies of the Scriptures." At that point all of his disciples ran away and abandoned him.*

The Bible says Jesus had an intense feeling of great sorrow plunged his soul into agony. And he said to them, "My heart is overwhelmed and crushed with grief. It feels as though I'm dying. Stay here and keep watch with me." What do you do with that? How do you not just crumble hearing those words? Our Jesus was crushed with grief. He felt like he was dying. Ugh! The weight of what He was about to go through was extremely heavy. Words could not describe this level of agony.

Luke describes Jesus as sweating like drops of blood to the ground. Many scholars disagree as to the wording here being literal or figurative. Some think that Jesus actually dropped sweats of blood with the heaviness. What a picture of pain and agony carrying the burden of the world! Others think that it was more descriptive of the drops of sweat falling to the ground similar to drops of blood falling. We won't know for sure until we meet Jesus face to face. Jesus told His Father if there was another way to take this from Him but His will be done. What He wants is not important. This is the place we need to try to arrive at. For us, nothing is as important as Jesus. He is not our ATM machine. He is our Lord God. He is our Savior. He is the Anointed One.

Each and every time Jesus came back to the disciples, they were asleep. Jesus said their spirit was willing, but their flesh was weak. Jesus wanted the disciples to pray. He knew what he was about to endure. He needed their support. He got slumbering men. Jesus knew Judas would be there soon. Jesus kept going off to pray. Shaking. The heaviness overwhelming. Jesus could have called his angels to take Him away. He could have said no, I am not going to do it. I am not going through that. It's just not worth it. I saw the world throughout the years, and they are not worth it.

Thank you, Jesus you did not think that or do that! His love for us pushed Him forward. His compassion for us carried Him through every second. All of us, including Judas. Here he came. Judas walked up to Jesus with a large crowd of armed men. He kissed the cheeks of Jesus. This signified He was Jesus. Jesus said, "My beloved friend, is this why you've come.?" It was a heart-broken statement of Jesus. He was heart-broken that Judas would betray Him like this.

I love what John wrote about this part of the story. In John 18, they were asked by Jesus who they wanted. They replied Jesus of Nazareth. Jesus replied, "I am he." They drew back and fell to the ground. What a scene! Jesus spoke 3 simple words, "I am He." and they fell to the ground. How powerful! How powerful are those words spoken by Jesus? Could you imagine the scene? The crowd of people falling to the ground. Was there a rumble like thunder? What were they thinking when they were picking themselves off the ground? This is my awe and wonder moment. Jesus said I am He and they all fell to the ground. The power behind his words.

## 16

## Condemned by Jewish leaders & Peter's denial part 2

Jesus was about to go through horrific things here in Matthew 26.

*Matt 26- TPT* [57] *Those who arrested Jesus led him away to Caiaphas, the chief priest, and to a meeting where the religious scholars and the supreme Jewish council were already assembled.* [58] *Now, Peter had followed the mob from a distance all the way to the chief priest's courtyard. And after entering, he sat with the servants of the chief priest who had gathered there, waiting to see how things would unfold.* [59] *The chief priests and the entire supreme Jewish council of leaders were doing their best to bring false charges against Jesus, because they were looking for a reason to put him to death.*

[60] *Many false witnesses came forward, but the evidence could not be corroborated. Finally two men came forward* [61] *and declared, "This man said, 'I can destroy God's temple and build it again in three days!' "*

[62] *Then the chief priest stood up and said to Jesus, "Have you nothing to say about these allegations? Is what they're saying about you true?"* [63] *But Jesus remained silent before them. So the chief*

priest said to him, "I charge you under oath—in the name of the living God, tell us once and for all if you are the anointed Messiah, the Son of God!"

⁶⁴ Jesus answered him, "You just said it yourself. And more than that, you are about to see the Son of Man seated at the right hand of God, the Almighty. And one day you will also see the Son of Man coming in the heavenly clouds!"

⁶⁵ This infuriated the chief priest, and as an act of outrage, he tore his robe and shouted, "What blasphemy! No more witnesses are needed, for you heard this grievous blasphemy." ⁶⁶ Turning to the council he said, "Now, what is your verdict?"

"He's guilty and deserves the death penalty!" they answered. ⁶⁷ Then they spat on his face and slapped him. Others struck him over and over with their fists. ⁶⁸ Then they taunted him by saying, "Oh, Anointed One, prophesy to us! Tell us which one of us is about to hit you next?"

⁶⁹ Meanwhile, Peter was still sitting outside in the courtyard when a servant girl came up to him and said, "I recognize you. You were with Jesus the Galilean."

⁷⁰ In front of everyone Peter denied it and said, "I don't have a clue what you're talking about."

*71 Later, as he stood near the gateway of the courtyard, another servant girl noticed him and said, "I know this man is a follower of Jesus the Nazarene!"*

*72 Once again, Peter denied it, and with an oath he said, "I tell you, I don't know the man!"*

*73 A short time later, those standing nearby approached Peter and said, "We know you're one of his disciples—we can tell by your speech. Your Galilean accent gives you away!"*

*74 Peter denied it, and using profanity he said, "I don't know the man!" At that very moment the sound of a crowing rooster pierced the night. 75 Then Peter remembered the prophecy of Jesus, "Before the rooster crows you will have denied me three times." With a shattered heart, Peter left the courtyard, sobbing with bitter tears.*

Here we are. The mob asked if he was Jesus of Nazareth. Jesus pronounced, "I am He." The entire mob fell back to the ground. Once they got back up, they seized Jesus and arrested Him. Although, truth be told, Jesus allowed them to arrest Him. No force on Earth would be strong enough to seize Jesus without Him allowing it. One of the disciples pulled out a dagger and cut off the ear of one of the servants of the High Priest. Jesus told him to put the knife away. He stated that he could call legions of Angels to take him away but it would stop God's plan.

He willingly gave himself up to them. Jesus' statement to the mob then spoke of fulfilling the prophecies in scripture. Then all the disciples deserted Him. I often wonder why they all deserted Him. Was it because of fear of dying with Him? Was it because they figured he said this was going to happen and He is letting it happen so leave? What was going through their heads at this moment? Did the Holy Spirit lead them away to protect them knowing they had more work to do for Jesus? That is a question for Jesus one day.

Jesus was led away to Caiaphas and a council of Jewish leaders. Peter followed them quietly to observe and see how things unfold. He sat outside while Jesus was inside facing his accusers. The Religious Scholars and Supreme Jewish Council had been plotting to find a way to convict and murder Jesus. They were just looking for a reason. Many false witnesses spoke up, but none could be corroborated. The Chief Priest asked Jesus point blank if he had any statement against these allegations. Jesus remained silent. The Chief Priest asked him under oath, is he the Messiah, the Son of God? Jesus answered him, "You just said it yourself. And more than that, you are about to see the Son of Man seated at the right hand of God, the Almighty. And one day you will also see the Son of Man coming in the heavenly clouds!"

This powerful, amazing statement infuriated the Chief Priest. Imagine the scene. Jesus, the Messiah they had wished for their entire life. The Lamb of God prophesied in the Old Testament is standing in front of them. The Son of God that they taught about was there and they wanted to kill Him. They knew more than anyone what the Old Testament said about the coming Messiah, yet they did not see what was in front of them. Caiaphas tore his robe in disgust of what he thought was a blasphemer. Jesus a blasphemer? How could one be so far off? All the healings. All the miracles. All the deliverances. Everything that Jesus did, and they could not see who He was? I get it. A big part of it was their own arrogance. They thought Jesus couldn't possibly be the Messiah, Jesus didn't use them in all His miracles, healings, or deliverances.

Instead of using the Priests, the Jewish leaders, and more, He used sinners, fishermen, and men of low intelligence at least in the eyes of the Priests. Jesus chose men of passion, strength, love, and compassion. He did not choose men that wanted to look religious, look good to other men, or had no heart as Jesus. The Priests were determined to murder Jesus and they were not going to stop until they did. At this point, they pushed the death penalty for Jesus. They slapped Him. They spit on Him. They punched Him. They mocked Him. Jesus. Let me say that again. They slapped Jesus. They spit on Jesus. They punched Jesus. They mocked Jesus. How could anyone treat Jesus this way? How could Jesus take that? I admit, I couldn't. If I was in his shoes, I could not take it. He took it all and more.

My heart hurts when I think about the way he was treated. It would be nearly impossible to treat anyone this way. But Jesus?

During all of this horrible scene, outside this place was Peter. He was sitting in the crowd. I imagine he was hiding. There was a girl there that said he was with Jesus. Peter denied it. Later on, another girl said that Peter was a follower of Jesus. Peter denied it. A little while later, some people standing near Peter said that they recognized him, and he was a follower of Jesus. This time, he cussed, then Peter denied Him. At that moment, the sound of a crowing rooster pierced the night.

Peter denied Jesus three times. Just as Jesus said. All of his talk and when trouble came about, he did exactly what Jesus said he would do, deny Him. In my mind, this is worse than what they Jewish leaders had done up to this point. Right or wrong, it is my opinion. How could someone who was with Jesus daily for three years, saw everything He saw, loved Him as much as Peter did, yet deny Him? Again, I wonder if the Holy Spirit was protecting them knowing they had more work to do? Maybe. Was it out of fear? It is a great question to ask Jesus one day.

One of the awe and wonder moments here is Jesus's patience. Whether in the garden, betrayed by Judas, arrested by the mob, being slapped, punched, mocked, or denied, Jesus could have said enough. He could have called Angels to get Him, and He would have never gone through everything He went through. Each and every moment, each and every punch, slap, mock, and deny was an opportunity for Jesus to express His love for us. An opportunity to express how important we are to Him. Simply amazing!! What level of love would you have to have to accept all of this? I'm in awe of it.

I imagine that there was never a point where he even questioned if it was worth it. He love was so immense, so deep, so overwhelming that he never paused to think if it was worth it. If we are worth it. He knew they were, and we are! There are not even words in the English language yet to describe the level of love Jesus has for us. The next time you feel unloved, lonely, unworthy, useless, or unwanted, know that Jesus loves you that much! He loves all of us that much!!

## 17

## Jesus taken before Pilate

Things were about to get worse for Jesus. After getting spit on, beat on, slapped, mocked, and more, Jesus was about to be brought before Pilate.

*John 18-TPT* *²⁸ Before dawn they took Jesus from his trial before Caiaphas to the Roman governor's palace. Now the Jews refused to go into the Roman governor's residence to avoid ceremonial defilement before eating the Passover meal. ²⁹ So Pilate came outside where they waited and asked them pointedly, "Tell me, what exactly is the accusation that you bring against this man? What has he done?"*

*³⁰ They answered, "We wouldn't be coming here to hand over this 'criminal' to you if he wasn't guilty of some wrongdoing!"*

*³¹ Pilate said, "Very well, then you take him yourselves and go pass judgment on him according to your Jewish laws!"*

*But the Jewish leaders complained and said, "We don't have legal authority to put anyone to death. You should have him crucified!" ³² (This was to fulfill the words of Jesus when he predicted the manner of death that he would die.)*

*33 Upon hearing this, Pilate went back inside his palace and summoned Jesus. Looking him over, Pilate asked him, "Are you really the king of the Jews?"*

*34 Jesus replied, "Are you asking because you really want to know, or are you only asking this because others have said it about me?"*

*35 Pilate responded, "Only a Jew would care about this; do I look like a Jew? It's your own people and your religious leaders that have handed you over to me. So tell me, Jesus, what have you done wrong?"*

*36 Jesus looked at Pilate and said, "The royal power of my kingdom realm doesn't come from this world. If it did, then my followers would be fighting to the end to defend me from the Jewish leaders. My kingdom realm authority is not from this realm."*

*37 Then Pilate responded, "Oh, so then you are a king?"*

*"You are right." Jesus said, "I was born a King, and I have come into this world to prove what truth really is. And everyone who loves the truth will receive my words."*

*38 Pilate looked at Jesus and said, "What is truth?"*

*As silence filled the room, Pilate went back out to where the Jewish leaders were waiting and said to them, "He's not guilty. I couldn't even find one fault with him. 39 Now, you do know that we have a custom that I release one prisoner every year at Passover—shall I release your king—the king of the Jews?"*

*⁴⁰ They shouted out over and over, "No, not him! Give us Barabbas!" (Now Barabbas was a robber and a troublemaker.)*

**John 19- TPT** *19 Then Pilate ordered Jesus to be brutally beaten with a whip of leather straps embedded with metal. ² And the soldiers also wove thorn-branches into a crown and set it on his head and placed a purple robe over his shoulders. ³ Then, one by one, they came in front of him to mock him by saying, "Hail, to the king of the Jews!" And one after the other, they repeatedly punched him in the face.*

*⁴ Once more Pilate went out and said to the Jewish officials, "I will bring him out once more so that you know that I've found nothing wrong with him." ⁵ So when Jesus emerged, bleeding, wearing the purple robe and the crown of thorns on his head, Pilate said to them, "Look at him! Here is your man!"*

*⁶ No sooner did the high priests and the temple guards see Jesus that they all shouted in a frenzy, "Crucify him! Crucify him!"*

*Pilate replied, "You take him then and nail him to a cross yourselves! I told you—he's not guilty! I find no reason to condemn him."*

*⁷ The Jewish leaders shouted back, "But we have the Law! And according to our Law, he must die, because he claimed to be the Son of God!"*

*⁸ Then Pilate was greatly alarmed when he heard that Jesus claimed to be the Son of God! ⁹ So he took Jesus back inside and said to him, "Where have you come from?" But once again, silence filled the room. ¹⁰ Perplexed, Pilate said, "Are you going to play deaf? Don't you know that I have the power to grant you your freedom or nail you to a tree?"*

*¹¹ Jesus answered, "You would have no power over me at all, unless it was given to you from above. This is why the one who betrayed me is guilty of an even greater sin."*

*¹² From then on Pilate tried to find a way out of the situation and to set him free, but the Jewish authorities shouted him down: "If you let this man go, you're no friend of Caesar! Anyone who declares himself a king is an enemy of the emperor!"*

*¹³ So when Pilate heard this threat, he relented and had Jesus, who was torn and bleeding, brought outside. Then he went up the elevated stone platform and took his seat on the judgment bench— which in Aramaic is called Gabbatha, or "The Bench." ¹⁴ And it was now almost noon. And it was the same day they were preparing to slay the Passover lambs.*

*Then Pilate said to the Jewish officials, "Look! Here is your king!"*

*<sup>15</sup> But they screamed out, "Take him away! Take him away and crucify him!"*

*Pilate replied, "Shall I nail your king to a cross?"*

*The high priests answered, "We have no other king but Caesar!"*

*<sup>16</sup> Then Pilate handed Jesus over to them. So the soldiers seized him and took him away to be crucified.*

The Jews were using a particularly stern tone with Pilate. Pilate asked what crimes do they bring against this man. They responded, "We wouldn't be coming here to hand over this 'criminal' to you if he wasn't guilty of some wrongdoing!" Jesus, a criminal? I find it crazy that just a short time ago the Jews were welcoming Jesus into Jerusalem like a King. Now they are wanting to murder Him. Isn't it crazy how quickly people will turn on you? This is still true today. Some people will turn on you quicker than you can blink.

Pilate popped right back at them and told them to take Him and judge Him by Jewish laws then. That's when Pilate was told the reason they were there. They wanted to put Jesus to death. This was against their laws, but apparently, they were ok to put someone else up to doing it. This "criminal" was guilty of nothing, yet they wanted to kill him. To satisfy the Jews Pilate interrogated Jesus. Pilate asked Jesus if he was really the King of the Jews. Jesus's response was a question asking if it was him that wanted to know or just that others told him. Pilate said the obvious. He is not a Jew. He doesn't care about their religion.

Pilate asked Him point blank what He has done wrong. Jesus, of course, was perfect so the correct answer would be nothing. Jesus did not deny any wrongdoings. He knew it would not do any good. Everything He said just infuriated the Jewish leaders even more. Pilate was no exception. Jesus stated, "The royal power of my kingdom realm doesn't come from this world. If it did, then my followers would be fighting to the end to defend me from the Jewish leaders. My kingdom realm authority is not from this realm."

Jesus was stating Pilate had no power over him except what God gave him. Jesus was hyper focused on God's plan, and nothing was going to derail it. He was telling Pilate that Jesus was there because He wanted to be there not because of anything the Jews and/or the Romans have done. He was there because of His Father's will, not because He had done something wrong. Pilate said so you are a King? Then Jesus stated He was right. He was born a King, and was there to prove what truth really was. The truth was right in front of him, yet Pilate was asking what truth was. Jesus fulfilled all the prophecies of the Old Testament and brought them from this sounds good all the way to fact.

Pilate went back to the leaders and said he found no fault with Jesus. Not one fault. Pilate knew there would be a situation if he just let Jesus go so he decided to try to get them to say, "release

Him." He brought Barabbas, a known murderer and thief, in front of them in hopes that they would choose Jesus over Barabbas. I guess he thought surely, they would not chose a murderer over a blasphemer. They chose a murderer. A murderer over Jesus! A man who preaches love and compassion. A man that healed countless people. A man that delivered countless people from demons. A man that raised countless from the dead. He did nothing but good in the world, yet they wanted a murderer and thief over Him. Talk about heart-breaking!

Pilate finally agreed to have Jesus flogged. Jesus was beaten brutally with a whip of leather and metal strips. Let me say that again. **Jesus was beaten brutally with a whip of leather and metal strips.** That even sounds horrific. I could not even imagine the agony He went through. Each and every time that whip struck Him. Each and every time those metal strips gash into His skin. Some scholars say Jesus was whipped 39 times. Some say it is truly unknown. Obviously, that would be a question for Jesus at some point. However, they used the cat of nine tails with each of the 9 "tails" having a metal piece on it. If Jesus was whipped 39 times, then Jesus had those metal shards ripped into 351 times!!

The number 39 was an important but weird number. Why 39? Why not 40? Looking back at Roman beliefs, they recorded that they believed 39 times was as much as a man could take before death. Many that took that level of punishment even disemboweled themselves. In addition, Roman tradition is that flogging was their punishment. No other recording ever showed a person getting flogged to that point then crucified, except Jesus. In fact, Pilate stated several times that this man was innocent, and he did not want to kill him. He ordered Jesus to be flogged to pacify the Jewish leaders that were out for blood. Pilate even said that His blood is on their hands. While that statement is true, it is also false at the same time. The innocent person's blood was on the hands of the Jewish leaders as they were doing what they could to get Pilate to kill Jesus. They definitely had a part in what was happening, so that statement is true. However, that statement was false as well.

You see, once you know. Once you understand the truth. Once you see, you cannot wash it off. Once your eyes are open, you are not innocent. There is no denying it. No saying you did not know. Pilate was told by Jesus Himself He was the King of the Jews. He cannot claim ignorance. The same for us. Once we see! Once we know! Once we get a taste! Once our eyes are open. Once the truth is laid out before us, we cannot claim ignorance. There is no denying of the truth.

After that, the soldiers covered his head and took turns beating Him, mocking Him, saying prophecy as to who hit you. They also said, "All hail, the King of the Jews." They shoved a crown of thorns on his head. Mocking Him. Beating Him. Torturing Him. Again, at any moment Jesus could have said enough. He could have called for the Angels to rescue Him. His love for all of us poured out just as His blood poured out. Pilate brought Jesus out. He showed how beaten He was. Bleeding. Thorns in his head. I can imagine every part of Him was in excruciating pain. Beaten almost to death. There He was, standing before the Jewish leaders as they shouted Crucify Him!

Pilate stated Jesus's innocence to the Jewish people to no avail. He brought Jesus back inside. He asked Jesus where he came from. Jesus did not answer. Jesus told Him he had no authority over Him except what is given to him from God. At that point Pilate was trying to find a way to let Him go. The Jewish leaders would not have it. They knew if they could put the Roman concerns on him as not being a friend of Caesar and anyone that states he is a King is an enemy of the emperor. All the Roman leadership was afraid of failing the Emperor. Afraid of looking like they did not have control over the Jews. Pilate heard this and gave up.

My Awe and Wonder moment here is at this point, Jesus could have said, "No, I'm done. Why go through all of what I went through and all I am about to go through for people that don't even want me." He could have said forget them; it is not worth it. These people are not worth it. Thousands of years later, the people are not worth the cost. Thank you Lord He did not. He loved them more than we could ever understand. Jesus loves us more than mere words could describe. How could any person put up with what he put up with for all of us? So many people do not honor Him. They say He is dead. They say he doesn't exist. They live their life the way they want, never giving Jesus a second thought. Even many Christians, they go through the motions at church. They don't pour out their love on Him as He deserves. They don't raise their hands. They don't bow before Him. Nothing. I want to be like the woman with the alabaster jar. My tears washing His feet. I want to pour out my perfume on Him. Give until it costs me everything. Tell Him and show Him how much I love Him!

## 18

## Jesus on the Cross

If the beating, the mocking, the slapping, the spitting, and more wasn't enough, things were about to get worse for Jesus.

*John 19- TPT [17] Jesus carried his own cross out of the city to the place called "The Skull," which in Aramaic is Golgotha. [18] And there they nailed him to the cross. He was crucified, along with two others, one on each side with Jesus in the middle. [19-20] Pilate had them post a sign over the cross, which was written in three languages—Aramaic, Latin, and Greek. Many of the people of Jerusalem read the sign, for he was crucified near the city. The sign stated: "Jesus of Nazareth, the King of the Jews."*

*[21] But the chief priests of the Jews said to Pilate, "You must change the sign! Don't let it say, 'King of the Jews,' but rather—'he claimed to be the King of the Jews!' " [22] Pilate responded, "What I have written will remain!"*

*[23] Now when the soldiers crucified Jesus, they divided up his clothes into four shares, one for each of them. But his tunic was seamless, woven from the top to the bottom as a single garment. [24] So the soldiers said to each other, "Don't tear it—let's throw dice to see who gets it!" The soldiers did all of this not knowing they fulfilled the Scripture that says, "They divided my garments among them and gambled for my clothing."*

*25 Mary, Jesus' mother, was standing next to his cross, along with Mary's sister, Mary the wife of Clopas, and Mary Magdalene. 26 So when Jesus looked down and saw the disciple he loved standing with her, he said, "Mother, look—John will be a son to you." 27 Then he said, "John, look—she will be a mother to you!" From that day on, John accepted Mary into his home as one of his own family.*

*28 Jesus knew that his mission was accomplished, and to fulfill the Scripture, Jesus said: "I am thirsty."*

*29 A jar of sour wine was sitting nearby, so they soaked a sponge with it and put it on the stalk of hyssop and raised it to his lips. 30 When he had sipped the sour wine, he said, "It is finished, my bride!" Then he bowed his head and surrendered his spirit to God.*

*31 The Jewish leaders did not want the bodies of the victims to remain on the cross through the next day, since it was the day of preparation for a very important Sabbath. So they asked Pilate's permission to have the victims' legs broken to hasten their death and their bodies taken down before sunset. 32 So the soldiers broke the legs of the two men who were nailed there. 33 But when they came to Jesus, they realized that he had already died, so they decided not to break his legs. 34 But one of the soldiers took a spear and pierced Jesus' side, and blood and water gushed out.*

$^{35}$ *(I, John, do testify to the certainty of what took place, and I write the truth so that you might also believe.)* $^{36}$ *For all these things happened to fulfill the prophecies of the Scriptures:*

*"Not one of his bones will be broken," They will gaze on the one they have pierced!"*

Pilate ordered Jesus to be crucified. Jesus had to carry his cross. Scholars disagree as to the weight of the cross and varies between 100 and 300 pounds. Whatever the weight actually was, it would be very heavy for a normal adult male to carry. If you factor in that he was nearly beaten to death, Jesus carrying the cross the entire way is nearly impossible. What pushed Jesus was His love for His people and His love for us.

Pilate had a sign placed over Jesus stating He was the King of the Jews. That infuriated the Jewish leaders. The question is why did he do that? Was it because he wanted to taunt the Jewish leaders? Was it because he truly believed Jesus was who he says he was? Was it to be able to mock Jesus even more? No one truly knows. Pilate refused to change the sign. They gambled over Jesus's clothes. The people mocked Jesus saying he can tear the temple down but he cannot come down from the cross. They said He saved others but he cannot save himself.

Jesus went through all the pain of the nails in His hands and in His feet. He went through all of the agony for His people, yet they mocked Him. They beat Him. They hit him. They pushed Pilate to crucify Him. How could he do this? He could have stopped it but he didn't. He could have said it is not worth it, but he didn't. He could have said they are not worth it, but he didn't. I know. I said this earlier in the book, but it is important enough to repeat. To truly get this in you. His love for us is beyond describable.

An amazing story comes to us from Luke. He gave a little insight on the criminals that were crucified with Jesus. Both of them in the same situation. Both dying on the cross for their crimes. Both guilty. Both have the huge opportunity for forgiveness right next to them. Only one accepts it. The first criminal was ridiculing Jesus, asking Him what kind of Messiah would allow this to happen to Him. His final opportunity to ask for forgiveness and he is mocking Jesus. On the other cross, the second criminal took the opportunity. He told the first criminal, "Don't you fear God? You're about to die! We deserve to be condemned. We're just being repaid for what we've done. But this man—he's done nothing wrong!" Then he said, "I beg of you, Jesus, show me grace and take me with you into your *everlasting* kingdom!" Jesus responded, "I promise you—this very day you will enter paradise with me."

Absolutely amazing! All the agony that Jesus was in. The torture that Jesus had gone through and still going through. The blood that Jesus had shed. The weight of the world on His shoulders. Yet Jesus still had the compassion and love for someone begging for

His forgiveness. The criminal knew he was a sinner. The criminal knew he was going to die. The criminal knew who Jesus was. He knew this was his last opportunity. He was at the Savior's mercy and His mercy knows no end. Here Jesus was at his weakest moment, yet Jesus's power of forgiveness and mercy was shown, one more time. Jesus was on the cross for 6 hours. That had to be the longest 6 hours anyone could ever imagine.

So, what happens when you are crucified? Suffocation, loss of body fluids, and multiple organ failures to summarize it. The heart and lungs would stop working as blood seeped out the wounds. The Guardian described it like this. Seven-inch nails would be driven through the wrists so that the bones there could support the body's weight. The nail would sever the median nerve, which not only caused immense pain but would have paralyzed the victim's hands. The feet were nailed to the upright part of the crucifix, so that the knees were bent at around 45 degrees. To speed death, executioners would often break the legs of their victims to give no chance of using their thigh muscles as support. It was probably unnecessary, as their strength would not have lasted more than a few minutes even if they were unharmed.

Once the legs gave out, the weight would be transferred to the arms, gradually dragging the shoulders from their sockets. The elbows and wrists would follow a few minutes later; by now, the arms would be six or seven inches longer. The victim would have no choice but to bear his weight on his chest. He would immediately have trouble breathing as the weight caused the rib cage to lift up and force him into an almost perpetual state of inhalation. Suffocation would usually follow, but the relief of death could also arrive in other ways. "The resultant lack of oxygen in the blood would cause damage to tissues and blood vessels, allowing fluid to diffuse out of the blood into tissues, including the lungs and the sac around the heart," says Ward. This would make the lungs stiffer and make breathing even more difficult, and the pressure around the heart would impair its pumping.

Unreal. How about you go back and read that description again? Let it sink in.

Words cannot describe how much Jesus went through. We can read the words, think about it, but never really could understand it fully. Keep in mind. He endured that for 6 hours. 6 hours! All for His people, for us, for you!

Luke talked more about the last moments of Jesus's life.

*Luke 23-TPT It was now only midday, yet the whole world became dark for three hours as the light of the sun faded away. And suddenly in the temple the thick veil hanging in the Holy Place was ripped in two! Then Jesus cried out with a loud voice, "Father, I surrender my Spirit into your hands." And he took his last breath and died.*

*[47] When the Roman captain overseeing the crucifixion witnessed all that took place, he was awestruck and glorified God. Acknowledging what they had done, he said, "I have no doubt; we just killed the righteous one."*

Jesus had been on the cross for 3 hours. Then the entire world became dark. Everything looked grim. I can imagine sadness roamed across the Earth. The Savior of the world was on his deathbed. The Messiah was on the cross. Beaten nearly to death. Slapped. Punched. Mocked. Flogged. Punched some more. Mocked some more. Nails driven into his hands. Nails driven into his feet. All seemed lost. Darkness fell across the Earth.

As Jesus proclaimed, "Father I surrender my spirit into your hands." and the veil in the Temple was ripped in two. The Earth shook violently. Rocks violently broke apart. At that point, the Roman Captain overseeing the crucifixion saw this, he said "There is no doubt, he was the Son of God." Another Roman Soldier now believes. The Jewish leaders did not want to have bodies on the cross on the day of preparation for the Sabbath, so they asked that their legs be broken to hasten their death. They broke the legs of the two criminals. They came to Jesus and saw he was already dead. To make sure, they took a spear and drove it into his side. Out poured blood and water.

What does that mean? Many scholars have discussed this. The most popular opinion is that the blood represents the redemption aspect. The water represents the life-imparting aspect. His blood was shed for forgiveness of sins. The water represents the new life that Jesus gives to anyone that asks for that forgiveness and takes Him as their Lord and Savior.

This was a difficult chapter to select an Awe and Wonder moment. There are so many. Since I must select one, I choose the part where the criminal is hanging on the cross next to Jesus. Guilty. Sinner. Criminal. Degenerate. What law did he break? We don't know. I'm sure Jesus did but it didn't matter at that point. All the suffering Jesus had gone through and was still going through, yet his love, his compassion, his mercy came out of Him yet again. He could have said, "Do you see where we are? Leave me alone!" or how about "I'm too weak" or maybe "he made his bed now he can lie in it." There are so many things he could have said, but he did not. The criminal begged Him for forgiveness. Jesus didn't even pause. He told Him he was forgiven. My awe and wonder moment is Jesus showing the ultimate example of love, mercy, and compassion for someone that did not deserve it. A valuable lesson to us all as we are all guilty and do not deserve His forgiveness, yet he freely gives it to us when we ask Him.

## 19

Jesus's burial and resurrection

The world was dark, grim. The death of Jesus had saddened everyone.

*John 19-20- TPT* <sup>38</sup> *After this, Joseph from the city of Ramah, who was a secret disciple of Jesus for fear of the Jewish authorities, asked Pilate if he could remove the body of Jesus. So Pilate granted him permission to remove the body from the cross.* <sup>39</sup> *Now Nicodemus, who had once come to Jesus privately at night, accompanied Joseph, and together they carried a significant amount of myrrh and aloes to the cross.* <sup>40</sup> *Then they took Jesus' body and wrapped it in strips of linen with the embalming spices according to the Jewish burial customs.* <sup>41</sup> *Near the place where Jesus was crucified was a garden, and in the garden there was a new tomb where no one had yet been laid to rest.* <sup>42</sup> *And because the Sabbath was approaching, and the tomb was nearby, that's where they laid the body of Jesus.*

*20 Very early Sunday morning, before sunrise, Mary Magdalene made her way to the tomb. And when she arrived she discovered that the stone that sealed the entrance to the tomb was moved away!* <sup>2</sup> *So she went running as fast as she could to go tell Peter and the other disciple, the one Jesus loved. She told them,*

*"They've taken the Lord's body from the tomb, and we don't know where he is!"*

*³ Then Peter and the other disciple jumped up and ran to the tomb to go see for themselves. ⁴ They started out together, but the other disciple outran Peter and reached the tomb first. ⁵ He didn't enter the tomb, but peeked in, and saw only the linen cloths lying there. ⁶ Then Peter came behind him and went right into the tomb. He too noticed the linen cloths lying there, ⁷ but the burial cloth that had been on Jesus' head had been rolled up and placed separate from the other cloths.*

*⁸ Then the other disciple who had reached the tomb first went in, and after one look, he believed! ⁹ For until then they hadn't understood the Scriptures that prophesied that he was destined to rise from the dead. ¹⁰ Puzzled, Peter and the other disciple then left and went back to their homes.*

*¹¹ Mary arrived back at the tomb, broken and sobbing. She stooped to peer inside, and through her tears ¹² she saw two angels in dazzling white robes, sitting where Jesus' body had been laid—one at the head and one at the feet!*

*¹³ "Dear woman, why are you crying?" they asked.*

*Mary answered, "They have taken away my Lord, and I don't know where they've laid him."*

*14 Then she turned around to leave, and there was Jesus standing in front of her, but she didn't realize that it was him!*

*15 He said to her, "Dear woman, why are you crying? Who are you looking for?"*

*Mary answered, thinking he was only the gardener, "Sir, if you have taken his body somewhere else, tell me, and I will go and . . ."*

*16 "Mary," Jesus interrupted her.*

*Turning to face him, she said, "Rabboni!" (Aramaic for "My teacher!")*

*17 Jesus cautioned her, "Mary, don't cling to me, for I haven't yet ascended to God, my Father. And he's not only my Father and God, but now he's your Father and your God! Now go to my brothers and tell them what I've told you, that I am ascending to my Father—and your Father, to my God—and your God!"*

*18 Then Mary Magdalene left to inform the disciples of her encounter with Jesus. "I have seen the Lord!" she told them. And she gave them his message.*

*19 That evening, the disciples gathered together, and because they were afraid of reprisals from the Jewish leaders, they had locked the doors. But suddenly Jesus appeared among them and said, "Peace to you!" 20 Then he showed them the wounds of his hands and his side—they were overjoyed to see the Lord with their own eyes!*

*21 Jesus repeated his greeting, "Peace to you!" And he told them, "Just as the Father has sent me, I'm now sending you." 22 Then, taking a deep breath, he blew on them and said, "Receive the Holy Spirit. 23 I send you to preach the forgiveness of sins—and people's sins will be forgiven. But if you don't proclaim the forgiveness of their sins, they will remain guilty."*

*24 One of the twelve wasn't present when Jesus appeared to them— it was Thomas, whose nickname was "the Twin." 25 So the disciples informed him, "We have seen the Lord with our own eyes!"*

*Still unconvinced, Thomas replied, "There's no way I'm going to believe this unless I personally see the wounds of the nails in his hands, touch them with my finger, and put my hand into the wound of his side where he was pierced!"*

*26 Then eight days later, Thomas and all the others were in the house together. And even though all the doors were locked, Jesus suddenly stood before them! "Peace to you," he said.*

*27 Then, looking into Thomas' eyes, he said, "Put your finger here in the wounds of my hands. Here—put your hand into my wounded side and see for yourself. Thomas, don't give in to your doubts any longer, just believe!"*

*28 Then the words spilled out of his heart—"You are my Lord, and you are my God!"*

*<sup>29</sup> Jesus responded, "Thomas, now that you've seen me, you believe. But there are those who have never seen me with their eyes but have believed in me with their hearts, and they will be blessed even more!"*

*<sup>30</sup> Jesus went on to do many more miraculous signs in the presence of his disciples, which are not even included in this book. <sup>31</sup> But all that is recorded here is so that you will fully believe that Jesus is the Anointed One, the Son of God, and that through your faith in him you will experience eternal life by the power of his name!*

Joseph and Nicodemus had to move quickly. They had to get Jesus down off the cross, his body prepared by Jewish customs, and buried in a short amount of time. His body had to be down before sunset. What was that like? Seeing Jesus's body as it was. All that he went through. What an honor to take care of Jesus's body and prep it for burial! It would truly be an honor to do so. Heart-breaking at the same time but an honor. I can't imagine the emotions of seeing Jesus's body like that, knowing He had died, what He went through, and the ability to take care of His body.

That Sunday morning, Mary Magdalene went to his tomb. Why? To put flowers around the tomb. To talk with Him. No one knows for sure. It does tell me that they were not convinced that Jesus would rise from the dead. If they were, why would she even go? I understand why she would be crying after seeing Jesus go through that but if she remembered what Jesus said, why would she go to the tomb? When she got there, the stone was rolled away. She ran back to Peter and John to tell them what she saw. She said, "They've taken the Lord's body from the tomb, and we don't know where he is!" It never crossed her mind that Jesus was alive. She thought someone stole his body.

Peter and John ran to the tomb. John, being faster got there first. He did not enter but merely peeked in. He saw the linens but no body. Peter caught up and blew by John, running directly into the tomb. Jesus's body was nowhere to be found. Did they think that Jesus rose from the dead? Jesus did everything he said he would, why wouldn't he do that? He said he would. He even specified three days. It had been three days, but Peter's feeble human mind could not comprehend Jesus being alive again. He just could not believe it, as much as He wanted to. The burial cloth that had been on Jesus' head was rolled up and placed away from the linen.

Then John spoke up and said that Jesus had risen from the dead, just as he said. John believed. Peter did not. He was puzzled. They went back home. Mary arrived back at the tomb sobbing and broken. Her Messiah was dead. Someone stole His body. She was dumbfounded but at the wrong thing. Through her tears, she saw two Angels in dazzling white robes, sitting at either end of where Jesus had laid. They asked her why she was crying. She said, "they have taken away my Lord, and I don't know where they laid

Him." If she only believed what Jesus said, she would have been celebrating Jesus's triumph over death. Instead, she was sobbing over Jesus's missing body.

She turned around and there stood Jesus in all His glory. She didn't realize it was Him. Jesus said, "Dear woman, why are you crying? Who are you looking for?" Mary answered, thinking he was only the gardener, "Sir, if you have taken his body somewhere else, tell me, and I will go and . . ."

"Mary," Jesus interrupted her.

Turning to face him, she said, "Rabboni!" (Aramaic for "My teacher!")

What a reunion! What a moment! Her sadness turned into joy. Her agony turned into celebration. Jesus is alive!! He defeated death! He took all of that punishment to death and rose again from the dead. His triumph over death is the greatest victory in all of history. Jesus stood in front of her with all His glory and all His majesty. What did Mary see? How did she feel seeing the King of Kings right in front of her, alive again? What is it like to hug Jesus? She grabbed him, clinging to Him. Wow! What was that like? To be able to cling to Jesus. Love on Him. I can imagine the tears just pouring down her face. The Savior, alive again! I have to admit, I would have a hard time letting Him go. I would want to wrap my arms around Him and not let go.

Mary ran back to tell the Disciples what she saw and what Jesus told her. Later that evening the Disciples gathered together. Jesus appeared to them saying, "Peace to you." What was that like? What were the Disciples thinking when they saw Jesus standing in front of them? All they saw. All they witnessed and this was the greatest miracle of all, right in front of their eyes. What did He look like? Was the glory of God all around Him? Did they fall down and worship Him? If not, how could they not? The true love of their lives is alive again, right in front of them. Did they celebrate? Did they have a party to end all parties? That would be some church service! Their Victor is alive! Death has been defeated! What a celebration that would be!

Then came the part of the story I love. Thomas. Doubting Thomas. He was not there that night. The Disciples came to him later and told him Jesus was alive. We saw Him! Still unconvinced, Thomas replied, "There's no way I'm going to believe this unless I personally see the wounds of the nails in his hands, touch them with my finger, and put my hand into the wound of his side where he was pierced!" You could hear the pain in those words. The pain of The Messiah being murdered.

Jesus appeared to him eight days later. Jesus said, "Put your finger here in the wounds of my hands. Here—put your hand into my wounded side and see for yourself. Thomas, don't give in to your doubts any longer, just believe!" Unreal! What was going through

Thomas's head seeing this? The wounds that he knew Jesus had, right in front of Him. All the doubt, gone. All the pain, gone. All the depression, gone. I can imagine he was trembling seeing what he was seeing. All the love. All the tears. They all came pouring out of him and he said, "You are my Lord, and you are my God!" I can imagine it was a loud proclamation. I don't think it was a small, quiet, statement. It poured out of him!

My Awe and Wonder moment for this chapter is John. The beloved of Jesus. Mary thought Jesus' body was stolen and was upset due to that. Peter was puzzled by Jesus's body not being there. Neither thought for a second that Jesus was risen. He even told them he was going to do it. They didn't believe it. He told them he would rise in three days. It had been three days. Yet, their human minds could not believe it. Not John. Not His beloved. John immediately knew he had risen from the dead. What faith! What level of faith would you have to have to proclaim Jesus was alive after seeing him crushed like He was? I imagine that his heart was racing, his excitement level was high, he knew Jesus was alive!

Did he call out for Him? Did he look around for Him? Knowing He was alive, did he spend any time looking for Him? Maybe. Maybe not. I am in awe of John in a few ways. One, to be listed in the Bible as Jesus' beloved. Jesus' beloved. Then to be the only one that believed from the beginning that Jesus was alive. The excitement. The awe and wonder of Jesus being alive again!

## 20

## Conclusion

We have lost the Awe and Wonder of Jesus. What Jesus did in the time he had on Earth was nothing short of amazing. His focus on His mission was phenomenal. He was not going to be stopped. His love for us was greater than any punishment he received. He knew His greater purpose. He was born for a reason. He was born to speak the truth. He was born to be a testament to the Glory of God. He was born to be a reflection of compassion and love for His people.

Looking at his birth, even Herod knew of His importance and feared Him. Herod murdered every male child 2 years and younger in Israel. They feared Him even before He was born. They feared losing their power, their control over people. Mary and Joseph knew of His importance. They knew he was not a normal baby. He was something special. Every time Mary or Joseph kissed the face of their baby, they were kissing the face of God. Every time they hugged their baby, they were hugging the Messiah. Did they know how many lives He was going to change? Did they know the mark that Jesus left on the Earth at that time? Did they know the impact that Jesus would make throughout history?

John the Baptist had the honor of baptizing Jesus. What an honor would that be! In reality, Jesus should have been baptizing everyone there, but Jesus wanted to be baptized. John the Baptist was the perfect choice. He was the forerunner. He was the one that comes before Jesus in Old Testament prophecy. He was the one that pointed out Jesus when he came to them. John told the crowd that Jesus was the Lamb of God. During that awe and wonder moment, all in attendance had the honor of hearing God's voice saying He was well pleased with His son Jesus. What did that sound like? Then Jesus was taken into the wilderness. What did that look like?

Then Satan tempted Jesus three times. Each time was a futile attempt to derail Jesus from His mission. Offering Him food since he had not eaten for forty days. The ironic thing is Jesus could create food any time he wanted. Then he tempted Jesus by testing his power and authority. Again, ironically, Jesus could have called His Angels at any time to save Him, yet that would go against His Father's plan. He loved us too much to not complete the mission. Then the funniest of all happened. Satan tried to tempt Jesus by giving Him all the kingdoms of the Earth. Satan did not own the kingdoms of this Earth, so it was not his to give.

If you look at nearly every healing, deliverance, and miracle that Jesus did, there were two common themes in all of them. One is compassion and the other is love. From raising Lazarus, raising the young girl, raising the young boy, healing the leper, healing the paralyzed man, feeding thousands, delivering the demonized, the adulteress, and many more. Every one of these stories was a reflection of Jesus's love and compassion for His people. Despite some that were out to kill him, his mercy, his love, and his compassion was greater.

We will never understand fully with our frail human minds, our human logic, opinions, and issues the level of love that Jesus has for us. His ways are higher than ours. He doesn't base his level of love for us based on what man does, says, or acts like. His love is a pure love that never changes. I just can't get past this thought that I talked about earlier a few times. He went through so much leading up to the cross from His people and the Romans. He was spit on, slapped, punched, mocked, and more from the Jewish leaders.

At any time, he could have said, enough. Enough is enough. Why go through this for people that are treating me this way? They are not worth it. Why take all of this from them and knowing what He was going to take from the Romans, why? Why would he go through this? His love and compassion for His people, the Romans, everyone across the world and throughout all of time, all of us. That is a love we could never fully understand. We would say forget them; they treat me like this. Why would I do this? Thankfully, he did not. Thankfully, Jesus's ways are higher than our ways. Thankfully, his compassion and love for us is greater than a few misguided people.

The Awe and Wonder of Jesus is very important in our walk with Him. We must see Him as our Lord. As our Savior. As our King. We must put Him on the throne in our own lives each and every day. Make Him the center point of our lives. When we do this, this is where we see His glory in everything around us. It is amazing that the one who created the Heavens and the Earth, the one who places the stars in the sky, the one that tells everything where to go, where to move, and where to be, the one that created all the animals, the one that blew life into man, loves us so much that he pursues us. He pursues our heart! He wants all of us and he knows the only way to get all of us is through our heart.

When we see the Glory of God all around us, we see everything differently. When Jesus becomes the center of our world, placed on His throne in our lives, and our heart is His, our lives will never be the same! Things will happen. Life happens. Sickness happens. Marriage problems. Money problems. Children problems. Job problems. Problems. Problems. Problems. They will always be there. They are just not as important when Jesus is most important of all. When we place 100% trust in Him. When we can stand up and say, "Jesus, whether you answer my prayer or not, YOU are still my Lord and Savior. You are still my provider. You are still my God. I live to serve you. I live to please you!!"

When we can reach that point, things change. Yes, he can still heal you. He can still heal your marriage. He can still bless you.

But the greater trust is knowing that Jesus will do what is in our best interest, no matter what. It may or may not be what we ask for, but it will always be what is best for us. That is a level of love we don't fully understand. As parents, we can understand to a point, but we will never fully understand it. This is another part of our level of faith, knowing that he loves us beyond our comprehension, that He will always do what is best for us, and that nothing will ever change that level of love for us.

You want to see the Awe and Wonder of Jesus. Start looking at the Glory of God all around you. Cut off the negative nellies on social media. Cut off the media who twist the news to fit their agenda. Set your focus on good. Set your focus on the glory of God in everything. Give Him praise and honor for everything. This must be an everyday thing. This is not a Sunday morning church thing. He deserves so much more than just a Sunday morning worship.

Each and every day worship Him. Sing praises to Him. Talk with Him. Give Him the glory for things that happen every day. Honor him with our words, our actions, and our attitudes. At church, then we come together as a family, and honor Him together. I guarantee if we as a church body would honor and glorify Him daily, our worship on Sunday would never be the same. The worship would be so heart-felt, so strong, so powerful, that Jesus would lean forward on His throne to listen. It would move His heart.

When we move His heart and connect His heart with our hearts, you will see the Awe and Wonder of Jesus. You will see miracles we have never seen before. You will see healings we have not seen before. You will see sides of Jesus we have not seen before. This will increase our Awe and Wonder of Jesus beyond any words could ever describe! This is my heart's cry! I want to see our hearts poured out for Him! Our love poured out for Him! Our desire for Jesus becomes greater than anything else! Jesus is the perfect example of giving everything. While we could never give everything that He gave, we can certainly give what we have to see the Awe and Wonder of Jesus radiate across the Earth!

# The Names of Jesus

**Advocate (1 John 2:1)**

**Almighty (Rev. 1:8; Mt. 28:18)**

**Alpha and Omega (Rev. 1:8; 22:13)**

**Amen (Rev. 3:14)**

**Apostle of our Profession (Heb. 3:1)**

**Atoning Sacrifice for our Sins (1 John 2:2)**

**Author of Life (Acts 3:15)**

**Author and Perfecter of our Faith (Heb. 12:2)**

**Author of Salvation (Heb. 2:10)**

**Beginning and End (Rev. 22:13)**

**Blessed and only Ruler (1 Tim. 6:15)**

**Bread of God (John 6:33)**

**Bread of Life (John 6:35; 6:48)**

**Bridegroom (Mt. 9:15)**

**Capstone (Acts 4:11; 1 Pet. 2:7)**

**Chief Cornerstone (Eph. 2:20)**

**Chief Shepherd (1 Pet. 5:4)**

**Christ (1 John 2:22)**

**Creator (John 1:3)**

**Deliverer (Rom. 11:26)**

**Eternal Life (1 John 1:2; 5:20)**

**Gate (John 10:9)**

**Faithful and True (Rev. 19:11)**

**Faithful Witness (Rev. 1:5)**

**Faithful and True Witness (Rev. 3:14)**

**First and Last (Rev. 1:17; 2:8; 22:13)**

**Firstborn From the Dead (Rev. 1:5)**

**Firstborn over all creation (Col. 1:15)**

**Gate (John 10:9)**

**God (John 1:1; 20:28; Heb. 1:8; Rom. 9:5; 2 Pet. 1:1;1 John 5:20;**

**etc.)**

**Good Shepherd (John 10:11,14)**

**Great Shepherd (Heb. 13:20)**

**Great High Priest (Heb. 4:14)**

**Head of the Church (Eph. 1:22; 4:15; 5:23)**

**Heir of all things (Heb. 1:2)**

**High Priest (Heb. 2:17)**

**Holy and True (Rev. 3:7)**

**Holy One (Acts 3:14)**

**Hope (1 Tim. 1:1)**

**Hope of Glory (Col. 1:27)**

**Horn of Salvation (Luke 1:69)**

**I Am (John 8:58)**

**Image of God (2 Cor. 4:4)**

**Immanuel (Mt. 1:23)**

**Judge of the living and the dead (Acts 10:42)**

**King Eternal (1 Tim. 1:17)**

King of Israel (John 1:49)

King of the Jews (Mt. 27:11)

King of kings (1 Tim 6:15; Rev. 19:16)

King of the Ages (Rev. 15:3)

Lamb (Rev. 13:8)

Lamb of God (John 1:29)

Lamb Without Blemish (1 Pet. 1:19)

Last Adam (1 Cor. 15:45)

Life (John 14:6; Col. 3:4)

Light of the World (John 8:12)

Lion of the Tribe of Judah (Rev. 5:5)

Living One (Rev. 1:18)

Living Stone (1 Pet. 2:4)

Lord (2 Pet. 2:20)

Lord of All (Acts 10:36)

Lord of Glory (1 Cor. 2:8)

**Lord of lords (Rev. 19:16)**

**Man from Heaven (1 Cor. 15:48)**

**Mediator of the New Covenant (Heb. 9:15)**

**Mighty God (Isa. 9:6)**

**Morning Star (Rev. 22:16)**

**Offspring of David (Rev. 22:16)**

**Only Begotten Son of God (John 1:18; 1 John 4:9)**

**Our Great God and Savior (Titus 2:13)**

**Our Holiness (1 Cor. 1:30)**

**Our Husband (2 Cor. 11:2)**

**Our Protection (2 Thess. 3:3)**

**Our Redemption (1 Cor. 1:30)**

**Our Righteousness (1 Cor. 1:30)**

**Our Sacrificed Passover Lamb (1 Cor. 5:7)**

**Power of God (1 Cor. 1:24)**

**Precious Cornerstone (1 Pet. 2:6)**

Prophet (Acts 3:22)

Rabbi (Mt. 26:25)

Resurrection and Life (John 11:25)

Righteous Branch (Jer. 23:5)

Righteous One (Acts 7:52; 1 John 2:1)

Rock (1 Cor. 10:4)

Root of David (Rev. 5:5; 22:16)

Ruler of God's Creation (Rev. 3:14)

Ruler of the Kings of the Earth (Rev. 1:5)

Savior (Eph. 5:23; Titus 1:4; 3:6; 2 Pet. 2:20)

Son of David (Lk. 18:39)

Son of God (John 1:49; Heb. 4:14)

Son of Man (Mt. 8:20)

Son of the Most High God (Lk. 1:32)

Source of Eternal Salvation for all who obey him (Heb. 5:9)

The One Mediator (1 Tim. 2:5)

**The Stone the builders rejected (Acts 4:11)**

**True Bread (John 6:32)**

**True Light (John 1:9)**

**True Vine (John 15:1)**

**Truth (John 1:14; 14:6)**

**Way (John 14:6)**

**Wisdom of God (1 Cor. 1:24)**

**Word (John 1:1)**

**Word of God (Rev. 19:13)**

**credit: The 100 names of Jesus from Faithful Sermons**

Made in the USA
Coppell, TX
24 April 2022

76977298R00105